PRIDE'S PURSUIT

CATHRYN FOX WRITING AS CAT KALEN

Cathryn
FOX
NEW YORK TIMES BESTSELLING AUTHOR

COPYRIGHT

Discover other titles by Cathryn Fox at www.cathrynfox.com. Please sign up for Cathryn's Newsletter for freebies, ebooks, news and contests:

https://app.mailerlite.com/webforms/landing/c1f8n1

ISBN 978-0-9878559-6-1

ISBN Print ISBN-13: 978-0-9878559-5-4

1

The fire has been burning for days, the savage blaze devouring everything in its drunken path. Wild, angry flames lick the star-studded sky as plumes of smoke form an eerie haze over the waxing moon, turning the night an ominous shade of red.

Chalky ash falls from the treetops like the winter's first snow and the scent of blood is so thick in the air it twists my stomach and clogs my dry throat. I wince as the bitter taste of death settles on the back of my tongue and burns my flesh like hot, molten silver.

At the crest of this secluded mountain town there are no fire trucks to be seen, no blaring alarms to be heard. Without a team of brave firefighters here to extinguish the inferno, I fear it could go on forever.

Hot panic is the first thing I feel. Anger is the second. It churns inside my gut, and the feral wolf inside me turns vicious as she takes in the senseless chaos unfolding before her eyes.

I breathe deep to move past the coppery tang of blood and smoke and that's when I catch a familiar scent, one that reminds me of rotten eggs and car exhaust. My pulse drums harder in my neck while my brain weeds through the smells, shifting and sorting until it's able to determine the true root of the odor.

Gasoline.

I give a hard shake of my head, my rattled brain struggling to come up with some plausible explanation as to who or what could have doused the village with fuel.

How was this secret town discovered?

I mull that over for a moment longer, and then suddenly my thoughts come to a screeching halt; the only reasonable answer lodging in my esophagus like a lump of day old bread.

"No," I cry out, my breath coming quicker now, the world around me blurring in and out of existence while waves of blistering heat wash over my trembling body. As the fire sucks the oxygen from the air, bile punches into my throat and it takes two locked knees to keep my legs from failing.

My hackles spike and a deep howl rents the air. The low-pitch sound chases the flames up the mountain only to get lost in the thick underbrush. Acrid smoke stings my eyes and I blink against its toxic bite as I quickly assess the damage. My head jerks from left to right and the brisk autumn breeze fueling the flames whips my curls across my face.

I push my hair from my watery eyes and strive to gather my thoughts. But before I can settle the chaos bouncing around inside my brain like a puppy's rubber chew toy, the shifters at my back bolt forward, leaving Logan and me alone in the bleak night.

A split second later—my father, Stone, Gem and Sandy—the wolves who travelled to Canada with Logan and me disappear from my line of sight, four brave warriors charging head first into the inferno. Even though I can't seem to move my legs, can't seem to follow them into the flames, the commotion pulls a reaction from my wolf.

Thick talons elongate, and her unchecked rage jumps a few notches, her animal instincts feeding off the dark destruction closing in on her. Deep inside she wails, clamoring to be unleashed. Her loud primal cry is a clear indication that she knows. She knows the person responsible for the destruction of Logan's entire village. His entire family.

That person is me.

While I might not have been the one to soak the village in gasoline, might not have been the one to ignite the match that lit the town on fire, I know this damage is my fault. I'm smart enough to understand this violence is a direct result of my escape from the compound a month ago, when the Paranormal Task Force chased me through Olympic National Park.

I have no doubt in my mind that the PTF officers—men who shoot first and ask questions later—tracked me to this private village, a place where werewolves live normal lives and take to the woods on shift night to avoid bloodshed.

It's the only logical explanation.

My hands fist at my sides and my heart pounds as rage unfurls inside me. This wasn't supposed to happen! None of this was supposed to happen. After freeing the pack of wolves trapped in our cruel master's cellar, six of us fled the California compound together and travelled to Logan's secluded home in the Canadian mountains with one purpose in mind.

To live normal lives.

But as I stare at the devastation, the complete and utter destruction of his entire community, I realize that as long as the PTF are out there, as long as they believe we are cold-blooded killers who feast on flesh and must be destroyed, we'll never be free.

I want to scream. I want to cry. I want to kill the officers who refuse to believe we can live normal lives. Refuse to believe we're not beasts, out to turn innocent humans into blood lusting monsters who kill for sport. What is it going to take for them to understand that we're not soulless predators?

I take a moment to process and when the full impact of what really happened here hits like a sucker punch, my stomach cramps and I nearly vomit. I swallow hard and my ears perk as dry tinder pops and splinters beneath the fiery assault, the sound reverberating off the distant, snow-packed peaks.

But soon the noise is drowned out by the deep, tortured howl coming from the boy beside me—a selfless boy who crawled straight into my hell to save me from certain death. I never should have drawn him into my dark world. If I hadn't accepted his help, the help of his family, then none of this would be happening.

When I see the horror in his blue eyes, and taste the bite of his fury as it pollutes the heavy air and mingles with black wisps of smoke, my anger turns to worry.

"Logan," I rush out, forcing my heavy legs to move so I can go to him. "Logan, I'm so sorry."

"You don't have anything to be sorry for." There is a definite edge to his voice, one fed by pure desperation, when he whispers through clenched teeth, "But whoever did this does."

Looking hard and dangerously feral, he angles his head unnaturally. Flecks of pewter puncture the blue in his eyes as they lock on mine, but judging from his wild, distant stare, I get the sense that it's not really me he's seeing.

The tormented look moving over his face is beyond frightening and as I take in the tension in his normally relaxed posture, equal amounts of fear and worry slither through my bloodstream like a poisonous snake. The truth is I've seen this boy beaten to within an inch of his life, yet never have I been so afraid for him.

Understanding his world is collapsing around him, I pinch back the tears stinging my eyes and touch his arm in an effort to bring his attention back to me.

"Logan," I say softly, knowing he may very well have lost everyone he's ever cared about and right now needs me to be the voice of calm, not anger. I temporarily shelve the rage inside me—a rage that is prompting me to find the men who did this and tear their heads clear from their bodies—so I can focus solely on what Logan needs from me.

"Pride," he whispers and pulls me to him. His hold is fierce, his embrace so tight it forces out what little oxygen I have left in my lungs. His voice echoes desperately inside my head as he buries his face in my disheveled hair. His breathing is rough, labored and I can feel his heart pound against my chest.

"Pride," he murmurs again, his voice shaking worse than his hands. I hold him tighter and can feel his enraged wolf prowling restlessly inside him, urging him to shift.

To kill.

"I'm here," I assure him, pain stabbing my heart like a double edged blade. I try to reach out to him mentally, to help soothe the dark distress eating him up inside. Despite our connection, an intimate bond that developed from trust while we struggled to survive together in the forest, I still can't speak to him telepathically.

"Everything is going to be okay," I say for lack of anything else, even though I know nothing is ever going to be okay again, especially if his entire family has been burned and left for dead.

When his hands fist my hair, my fingers curl in his t-shirt. The chaos around us fades to a distant buzz and as we cling to one another his warm familiar scent almost makes me feel safe. Almost.

As I offer whatever comfort I can, I listen to his blood

rush and despite the urgency of the situation we stay like that for a long moment, until a hard voice forces us to separate. I step back, but my wolf bristles, not wanting to break from Logan.

"*Pride*," Stone says, his deep guttural voice sweeping through my thoughts like the brush fire through the pines. I edge farther away from Logan, severing the connection as I turn to Stone.

He looks at me for a long moment, his eyes clouding with savage emotion before he says, "Y*our father wants you.*" Firelight illuminates his strong features as he speaks telepathically to me, a means of communication, I recently learned, that only true mates are capable of establishing while in their human form.

But now is not the time to be worrying about all the secrets that have been kept from me since birth, not when Logan's world is falling apart around him.

Stone inches closer, each step calculated, purposeful.

Predatory.

Fear shoots through me and the hairs on my nape prickle when I see worry tightening his features. His anxiety wraps around me like a lethal serpent and squeezes so hard I can feel my heart constrict to the point of pain.

I suck in a sharp breath and try not to cough as my lungs fill with smoke. "What is it?" I ask, forcing the words past my lips so I don't exclude Logan from our conversation.

He takes another measured step closer and I can feel the warmth of his body as his knuckles slide along mine. There is something very primal and raw in his eyes as they study me darkly. A moment passes before he finally answers me.

"We found someone. She's alive." His glance shifts to Logan and for the first time I don't see black hatred in his dark expression. And it's that lack of hatred that has me worried.

Stone, the alpha wolf who was destined to be my true mate, straightens to his full height and expands his chest as he makes eye contact with Logan, the boy I gave myself to—body and heart—during the last full moon.

Stone's forehead creases, the seriousness of the situation apparent in his expression. "You'd better come with us. She's asking for you."

Logan's eyes widen, a deadly tornado brewing in their stormy depths. "Who is it?" he rushes out.

"I don't know. She's not talking."

Logan makes a step to go, but Stone moves in front of him to block his path. His actions appear threatening to Logan's wolf, and I draw in a sharp breath when Logan assumes a combative stance.

With his body on edge, his every muscle tight, Stone searches the other boy's face. A hush falls over us, even the animals scurrying from the fire go mute as the two alphas glare at one another, their gazes clashing in a silent battle of wills. With my pulse jack hammering, I tense at the strained silence, and watch, transfixed, wondering what Stone is trying to prove.

This is not the time to be fighting for pack control!

But when he pitches his voice low and says, "She's hurt pretty badly," preparing his enemy for the horror he's about to face, my heart squeezes in my chest. Stone might be a hard alpha, a trained killer who's been caged and tortured his whole life, but deep inside he's just a boy.

One who is as lost as I am.

Logan gives a curt nod and when Stone steps back Logan takes the opportunity to bolt forward. I immediately chase after him and stay close, keeping pace as the grief-stricken alpha makes his way to his village. But soon his long legs are covering a vast amount of ground and I'm unable to keep up.

Stone lags behind and runs by my side, his shrewd eyes trained on my back. Watching me.

Always watching me.

Wind whips at my face as I steal a sideways glance at him. Speaking telepathically, I begin, *"Are they all...?"* But then I stop abruptly, unable to push any more words out. I don't need to finish the sentence for Stone to know what I'm asking, anyway. Even without making a mental connection, he can read my thoughts and actions as well as I can read his.

"I don't know. We only found the girl and she's not speaking."

I push harder, my feet slapping a steady beat against the hot road beneath me. Since we ditched our car long ago, not wanting to take a chance that my father's vehicle could be tracked to Logan's home, the final trek up the twisting mountain has to be made on foot.

The noise of my shoes pounding pavement echoes in the night and drowns out the hum of my heavy panting. Moisture breaks out on my skin, and my heart begins to beat so fast I fear it's going to burst from my chest. But I don't let that stop me. I can't. Worry for Logan and what he might find prompts me to dig my heels in deeper. There is no way I'm going to let him face this senseless brutality alone.

Just because I recently distanced myself from the alphas —deciding for all our sakes that I need to find myself and learn about my past before I can commit to my future—it doesn't mean that I don't care for the two boys. I do.

A lot.

We breeze by an abandoned playground. The rusty hinges on the old swing set squeal like a wounded animal as it sways in the night breeze. My heart clenches when I think of the children, a community lost, destroyed by cruel men who fear what they don't know. What they don't understand.

From everything I've witnessed over the last few weeks, it's become glaringly apparent to me that the PTF are nothing but trained assassins, more merciless than the wolves they hunt.

Then again, I can't forget about the one officer who saved my life after I spared his. But I very much doubt he can change the minds of many, not without some sort of proof that we're not simply out for blood. But how can we prove that, and how many more will die until we find a way?

My steps slow and Logan's hushed voice cuts through the chaos and reaches my ears as we approach a burned out building. Before I push my way into one of the fire-ravaged structures, Stone catches my hand in a firm hold.

My gaze darts to his and when his brow creases in concern, I note the ways his muscles are bunching, rippling along his shoulders and down his arms. His jaw seesaws from side to side, and I instantly brace myself, because I know that look.

I know what it means.

He inches closer, his body crowding mine. "I don't think you should go in," he warns.

I give a fierce shake of my head and my teeth clamp hard enough to chip bone. "Well I think I should," I counter and snatch my hand back from his tight grip.

While I understand it's in Stone's nature to protect me, and I wouldn't be alive today without his intelligence or sheer strength of character, he needs to understand that in the outside world, he can no longer be my strength.

I love and admire him for his protectiveness and intellect, I really do. And while I know he's a creature of habit, ruled by his survival instincts, I also know if we are going to thrive in a place where compound rules no longer apply, he has to allow me to grow, to find my path, and to respect my choices instead of trying to make them for me.

Looking rattled, he rakes his hands through his mussed

hair and everything inside me reaches out to him, my heart aching for the tormented alpha and all he's been through.

"*Pride*—" he begins, his voice a low, strained whisper as he makes a mental connection, and I instantly harden myself.

Knowing it's for Stone's own good—the good of our kind —I tilt my chin and glare at him with stubborn determination.

"This isn't up for debate," I say, my voice low, but unwavering.

He glares at me, then understanding I'm not about to back down, he disengages himself from my thoughts and gives a resigned shake of his head. Still I know he'll follow me.

With that I turn and push a broken and charred door out of my way. It falls to the floor and the noise shudders in the unnatural silence. Instincts on high alert, I step inside and my taste buds are instantly assaulted with the decaying stench of charred flesh. My gut clenches and my wolf howls in response, the smell so overwhelming that I have to breathe through my mouth to avoid choking.

Pushing on, I carefully pick my way through burnt debris, my feet falling mutely as I step over black beams and scorched floorboards. The house is dark, all but destroyed, the rooms lit only by the few orange embers still smoldering in the structure's outer edges.

With my senses guiding the way, I go deeper into the house, or at least what's still standing of it. The floor creaks and I fear it's about to collapse beneath Stone's impressive weight. He keeps close to me, so close I can feel his warm breath on my neck. We continue forward until I find the others in a room that once served as a kitchen.

Dread takes hold when I see a badly beaten girl—one who is no older than me. Crouched on the floor with her back braced against a seared wall, her breath is coming in quick, labored bursts.

Everything from the vacant look in her pale blue eyes, to the way her legs are pulled to her chest, her arms hugging them tightly against her bloody body, warns that she's still paralyzed with fear. The sour stench of her terror, a pungent mixture of curdled milk and spoiled meat, has the animal in me howling with rage, eager to seek revenge on those who did this to her.

As I pull in the scent, allowing it to fuel my wolf, Logan kneels in front of her. Talking in soft, whispered words he carefully brushes her ragged hair from her face. My perked ears enable me to listen in on the hushed conversation.

Not wanting to startle the girl I move in beside my father. I tilt my head to meet his glance and when I do his dark eyes narrow in genuine concern. After we exchange a worried look, I take in the stricken expressions of the other shifters in our pack. When my glance meets Gem's I gesture with a nod to Sandy, who looks paler than ever as she rubs the small bulge in her expanding belly.

Knowing this is no place for a girl in her condition and that her growing child shouldn't be exposed to any of the toxic fumes still lingering in the air, I jerk my head toward the doorway.

Gem instantly understands my message and leads Sandy outside. Once she's gone, I turn my attention back to Logan. Driven by pure instinct, I take a small step closer to him, my wolf needing in the most desperate ways to support the alpha she mated with. But when I do, the girl flinches. Undisguised panic ripples through her, and she pulls Logan against her, shielding her body with his.

"It's okay, Nova," he murmurs as he slides me a look that speaks volumes. While we might not be able to speak mentally, I know him well enough to understand what he's asking of me. I give a tight nod and inch back until I'm once again standing next to my father. After giving Logan and the girl a generous amount of space, Nova relaxes slightly, but she still doesn't ease her hold on the alpha.

"It's Pride," he explains, his voice both soft and soothing as he settles his own emotions so he can concentrate on Nova. My heart lurches, remembering all the techniques this boy once used to relieve my worries and gain my trust. While he might be young, his intuition and inner strength never fail to amaze me. "You remember Pride, don't you?" he asks.

Nova's jerky nod takes me by surprise. Her thick, death-black hair falls forward and masks her features as I study her harder, struggling to figure out who she is, and how she knows me. Before the answer comes to me, Logan slowly climbs to his feet, and his voice gives way to soft persuasion as he coaxes her to follow him up.

Her bones crack in protest as she stands and I wonder how long she's been crouched in that same position. Looking badly beaten and frightened to the point of tears her eyes rake over the motley crew with detached interest. But when her glance lands on me and lingers for longer than what's comfortable, I get the strangest sense that she's sizing me up.

Unease moves into my stomach and my hackles bristle. The dark warning shivering through my blood has my wolf growling. But I place my hand over my stomach to hush her.

Logan curls a protective arm around the girl's shoulders and pulls her against him to offer comfort. She melts into him and that's when her identity hits me. I'd briefly met her at Logan's house when he first introduced me to the members of his pack. That was close to four weeks ago, right after the last full moon—which, I can tell from the gnawing ache pulling at my joints, will be upon us again any day now.

But thinking about Logan's family has me worrying about Malcolm and the others who disappeared outside the master's mansion. I swallow the knot tightening my throat and wonder if they were involved in this bloodbath, or if they're still missing, either caught by the PTF or on the run from deadly, shape shifting panthers in California wine country.

"We can't stay here," Logan says quietly as he moves past my father and me to lead Nova outdoors. The hard lines on his face soften and there is real relief in his eyes when he lowers his voice and adds, "Nova said most of our pack made it out alive. Some might even be at our den just over that peak." He stops to jut his chin toward the eastern mountain. "She has more information but right now she's in no shape to talk. She has to shift and heal herself first."

As I watch them step over the rubble, and make their way through the crumbling house, I get the oddest feeling that something's not quite right here. Heightening my senses, I listen to Nova's blood pulse effortlessly through her veins. As I take in the smooth, unrestricted flow, I quickly conclude that the steady, rhythmic beat of her heart belies her stricken expression. Maybe she's not quite as frightened as she seems.

When Logan disappears around the corner with her packaged in his arms, I think about canine self preservation. While I understand that she's been through a great amount of trauma, I also understand shifting to heal is as inherent as breathing—so why hasn't Nova done it already?

What has her wolf been waiting for?

2

With my lungs starved for fresh mountain air, I shelve that thought to consider later and follow my father outside. We step into a clearing and as he makes his way toward the others I move past the smoke and catch a familiar scent in the night breeze. It's that element of danger fluttering by in the wind that torments my primal side and warns me to proceed with caution.

Stopping in my tracks, I breathe deep to pull the rich aroma of the forest into my lungs. I sort through nature's smells and a measure of relief moves through me when I detect traces of rain inching in from the west, but when I get the eerie sense that someone is watching me it troubles my restless wolf.

I shoot a glance around. Despite the heat from the fire, an uneasy feeling trickles along my spine and elicits a shiver from deep within. I wrap my arms around myself and continue to scan my surroundings, looking for possible threats, and unknown enemies.

I narrow my eyes and through imaginary crosshairs I capture Logan leading Nova toward the towering trees fringing the village. With undisguised sympathy etched on his face, he keeps her close, protected, holding her battered body tight against his. From my distance I can't hear what he's saying to her, but from the way her pale eyes watch him intently, to the way her body never once flinches, I can tell it's something very important.

I make a move to go toward them but when warm, rough knuckles brush along the small of my back it stills my steps and anchors me in place.

"*You okay?*" Stone asks, and I jump at the sound of his voice inside my head.

"*Yes,*" I answer quickly, and throw up a wall of defense to hide my private thoughts from him. I don't want him to worry about me any more than he already does. Besides, we have more troubling matters at hand. Like where are we going to find the monsters responsible for this deadly firestorm and what is it going to take for us to stop them from ever doing it again?

Thinking of the PTF has me sniffing the air again and wondering if we're alone. Could they be out there watching, waiting for us to lead them to the wolves who managed to flee their lethal fire? Their poisonous silver? Could they be waiting for us all to gather in one place so they can make a nice tidy kill using as little of their resources as possible?

Astute wolf that he is and able to read me better than almost anyone else, Stone's nostrils flare and he answers my unasked question, "*I think they're gone, Pride.*"

Understanding I can't hide much from his piercing eyes, I give an uneasy nod, then, when I see my father talking to Gem and Sandy, I start toward him. With determined strides I quickly close the distance but when Gem looks at me, my heart drops to my stomach. The pain beneath her glittering green eyes is a reminder that she's part of Logan's pack and this is—was—her home, too.

An apology lingers on my tongue. I want to tell her I'm sorry, that I plan to do whatever it takes to right this wrong, but I know she doesn't want sympathy from me. And like Logan she'd never hold me accountable for the destruction.

Regardless, whether they believe this is my fault or not, I know I'm the one responsible, and I know I have to do something about it.

"Logan mentioned a den," I say, sounding more in control than I feel.

Gem points to a distant peak, and I note how both fear and worry have dulled the shine in her eyes. "Up there."

I peer into the night, and wonder if any of her family actually made it there alive. Or could the PTF have tracked them up the mountain, to finish what they started? Since there is no sign of a fire, no smoke signals in the sky, I cling to the hope that they're safe and alive.

Somewhere in the near distance a nocturnal animal lets loose a wounded cry and all heads turn in its direction. Looking spooked, Sandy glances around nervously, her dark cautious eyes searching the forest as she inches closer to me.

I pull her against my body to offer comfort, and feel a measure of hope that she's going to be okay after all the trauma she's been through. I'm grateful that she no longer hates me, and that she now knows I'll do whatever it takes to keep her and her unborn safe.

But thinking about her baby has me wondering about the father, and where he might be now. It saddens me to think she was forced to mate with someone she didn't care for and I wonder what she'll feel for an offspring that wasn't created out of love. Will they bond, or will the child simply be a reminder of the harsh life we were forced to endure?

The master's cruel smile flashes in my mind's eye and my anger spikes. But then I remember the way I left him, in a faceoff with two deadly panthers out for blood. It's that memory that gives me a sense of relief, because I know he can never hurt any of us again.

A low whimpering sound escapes from Sandy's throat. "Everything is going to be okay," I say to soothe her and run my hand up and down her arm to create warmth. Beneath the fear I see in her eyes, I catch a glimpse of an emotion I can't quite identify, and it has my hackles spiking. A sad look pulls her mouth down, and I get the sense she wants to tell me something. I hug her tighter, and can feel her heart racing against her chest.

"What is it?" I ask gently, and take another glance around to see what has her so spooked.

Her eyes go so wide they look like they're ready to pop from their sockets. "He could be here," she whispers low, her shoulders slumping as her body closes in on itself, like she's trying to make herself smaller, invisible, the way we used to do when we were pups and the master was on a rampage.

"Who could be here, Sandy?"

"The master," she says weakly. A cold shiver wracks her body as she leans forward to let a curtain of wheat-colored hair hide her face. My nerves come alive because I get the oddest sense that she can't bring herself to meet my eyes. What is she ashamed of? That a cruel man managed to break her? Breed her with a powerful wolf so he could harness her offspring?

Or is it something else?

Either way, it's time to think about our future, not dwell on our past.

"He's gone," I assure her, and tuck a long strand of hair behind her ear to expose her face. I look into her worried eyes. "He can't hurt you anymore."

"What if—"

"There are no what ifs," I say in a bid to calm her. "He died at the hands of his enemies, Sandy. No human, no matter how cruel and powerful he is, can come back from an attack like that."

A strangled, gargle sound catches in her throat, and when anxiety bursts from her pores and explodes in the air like a pack of fireworks, it has my wolf howling, feeding off the intensity of her emotions. As I watch Sandy's peculiar reactions it has me wondering what I said to cause such a powerful response in her.

Sandy nibbles on her lips, like she wants to say more. But then stops herself and scrapes her front teeth over her mouth until her bottom lip is red and swollen. Practically bleeding.

Gem, who has taken on the big sister role to Sandy, tips her chin and says, "We should go."

When Sandy steps away from me, my stomach tightens with a mixture of apprehension and curiosity, and I make a mental note to get to the bottom of matters with her, right after I get us all to safety.

Modesty aside, Gem begins to unbutton her shirt and that's when I notice Logan and Nova, both shrouded in darkness beneath a sheltering oak tree. The way Logan is caring for Nova, helping the young wolf from her clothes, doesn't go unnoticed by me. Nor does the ugly sting of jealousy zinging through my bloodstream.

A low growl rumbles in the back of my throat, and I can't deny that the sight of the two standing so close taunts my wolf in primal ways. Blood lust rips through my veins, and my talons lengthen, but I diligently fight off the change, hating myself for allowing my wolf to feel threatened in the first place. Logan is a protector, an alpha, and he's only doing what comes natural to him.

I briefly shut my eyes to gain control over my emotions, something I find harder and harder to do as I work to become less animal and more human. Once calm, I take a moment to see the world through Nova's eyes, to consider her situation.

Unlike Stone and me, two wolves who've grown accustomed to brutality and bloodshed, Nova has never suffered abuse at the hands of a cruel master, has never been forced to witness such shocking violence. None of this can be easy for her.

I take a moment to play out the carnage she undoubtedly witnessed and I berate myself for my girlish behavior, for allowing my wolf to feel possessive under these horrifying circumstances. But I still can't seem to shake the uneasy feeling that there is more going on with the young wolf than meets the eye.

The sound of Stone moving in beside me pulls my focus and helps me to redirect my thoughts.

I give a hard shake of my head to clear it, and work to focus on the crisis at hand. "Are we travelling in wolf form?" I ask Gem.

"It's easier to get up the mountain that way, and we have clothes and food stashed at the den."

I nod and stand back while they finish stripping their clothes from their bodies and shift. Once they're all in their primal form, I gather their abandoned apparel and toss them into the fire for safe measure.

My mind briefly flashes to the vicious, shape shifting panthers that attacked us at the master's compound. I have no idea where they bunker down at night, or if the PTF can get them under control, but I'm not taking any chances that they can be harnessed and used to track us. When the clothes ignite, I tear my shirt and pants from my body and add them to the flames.

Standing naked beneath the near full moon, the blaze backlighting me from behind, I call on my wolf. But as my bones shift and slide into place, my young girlish screams turning to dark wolfish howls, I don't miss the powerful, streamlined wolf standing in the shadows.

Watching me.

His big beefy paws rake the ground, tilling the dirt and soil beneath his deadly nails. His nostrils flare, and silver eyes move over my frame as I drop to all fours. I canter toward him and he makes a deep throaty noise.

When I approach he nudges me with his muzzle, and I don't misinterpret the intimacy in his actions. He growls low into the fire ravaged night, then rubs up against me, interacting the way fated mates would. I look past his shoulder and swallow uneasily when I catch Logan studying us darkly.

The orange glow from the fire highlights the pewter in Logan's eyes. His growl is deep and menacing, his gaze sliding over me darkly. He continues to pace by the tree line, and his movements are purposeful, showcasing his powerful, streamlined body as he waits for me to make the next move.

I don't miss the strain in his eyes, a reminder that he's a pack alpha, a wolf who carries a world's worth of responsibilities on his shoulders. Even though he's still a boy, he's as loyal as a bloodhound to those he cares about. I sense his impatience with this whole mating situation, but I appreciate the fact that he is giving me the distance I need to find my way in this new world.

My mind briefly flashes back to the compound, to when I took comfort in Stone's arms during a moment of weakness. Guilt eats at me, my heart aching from my betrayal.

Driven by a need only my wolf understands, I take a step toward Logan, but when Nova's distressed howl cuts the silence, his whole body stiffens. A moment of hesitation passes over his eyes, then he gives one last glance my way before he darts up the mountain after the injured wolf. With a swish of my tail I go after them, Stone keeping watch over me from behind.

Swift on all fours, I advance on them, only to find Nova cantering happily alongside Logan. I cut her a curious glance but she doesn't return it. Hurrying my strides I move past her and wonder, was her distress howl simply a delayed reaction to the massacre she'd witnessed?

Or was there another purpose behind it?

I go higher up the mountain, and soon enough the soil beneath my feet turns to snow. Twenty minutes later, after reaching the eastern tip of the hill, we all gather outside a small cabin. I draw the night air into my lungs and my paws leave tracks in the dense snow as I walk the perimeter and search for signs of life. When I find none, I circle back to the others and that's when I notice the worry dancing in Logan's silver eyes.

I nudge him with my muzzle. *"Maybe they went farther,"* I say and glance down the mountain to see flames licking the sky. *"Maybe they didn't think it was safe being this close."*

"Maybe," Logan says and as he shifts back to human another thought hits and I wonder why I haven't considered it before.

There must be other hidden communities around the globe. Other wolves who live normal lives and take to the woods on shift night. Logan's pack can't be the only one. I make a mental note to ask him about this theory when we're alone.

As Logan uses his shoulder to push open the door everyone takes that opportunity to morph. When we do, the cool mountain air nips at our naked human flesh and Gem hurries us all inside before we get frostbite.

She rifles through a small dresser and distributes clothes. I pull on a pair of oversized sweat pants and a gray sweat shirt with University of British Columbia emblazed across the front. While everyone dresses, I use that time to catalogue my surroundings, looking for signs of danger in the cozy den designed for two, not seven.

I take in the small kitchen, the meager furnishings, and the single window with its majestic view of the night sky. Nostrils flaring, I pull the clean scent of pine needles and the fragrant aroma of freshly laundered bedding deep into my lungs. My nose crinkles and I wonder what this place is used for, but when my glance lands on the soft bed, and the fluffy pillows tossed haphazardly about, I don't need to ask to know.

Years ago when Jace and Clover—the elders I used to bunk with before they were brutally murdered because of my disobedience—thought I was asleep, I listened in on their private conversations. I remember overhearing them reminisce about what life was like life before capture. They talked about wolf customs and the special, isolated place two shifters would go for their first full moon mating. After another quick scan of the den, I'm convinced I'm in such a place.

My gaze instantly darts to Logan, my mind remembering the intimacies we shared in the cave the night the moon was full, when he saved me from myself. But that night was about so much more than Logan protecting nearby backpackers from my feral wolf, and I'll never forget what he asked of me that night, what I freely gave to him. Nor will I forget the implications in our actions and what it means to a pack.

From across the small room our eyes meet and lock. Everything in the way he's looking back at me, his eyes full of unchecked emotions, tells me he's thinking about that night, too. I reach out to him telepathically but when my call goes unanswered it simply reminds me that we were never destined to be mates.

That dark thought has my hackles bristling and I turn my attention to Nova as she steps in front of me, blocking my view of Logan. My gaze rakes over her tall, curvaceous body, now healed from her shift, and I tilt my head to meet her gaze unflinchingly.

Her lips peel back to expose white teeth but her smile holds no warmth. Pale blue eyes as cold as the dead of winter meet mine and she opens her mouth like she's about to say something, but her words never come.

"Nova," Logan says softly and slips his hand around her slim waist, illustrating his protectiveness of those in his care. With that, she pinches her lips shut and turns adoring eyes on her pack's alpha.

Logan's mouth tightens in genuine concern as he guides her to the sofa. He sits beside her and I don't miss the possessive way she looks up at him. While I know he's the alpha, respected and admired by all, I can tell that he's especially meaningful to her. I think back to the time that Logan told me his name means hollow, like a tree hollow or branch, one that provides a habitat for others. He's a protector and I know he doesn't take his role in the pack lightly.

His voice is low, quiet when he asks, "Do you think you're ready to talk?"

When she nods, Stone and my father move to stand by the small kitchenette counter while Gem, Sandy and I perch on the edge of the cushy mattress. With all eyes trained on Nova we sit quietly and listen as Logan asks the question I'm most anxious to hear.

"Did Malcolm and the others find their way back here?"

When she answers with no, her words ring hollowly in my head and I don't know whether to feel worry or relief. The fact that Malcolm and his small army haven't made it back means they weren't part of the carnage. But it also means they are still out there somewhere, either caught by the PTF or running from ferocious panthers.

Either way, if there is a chance they're still alive, I have to go back to help. And while I'm there, maybe I can convince the PTF that we're not what they think we are, and that we can be productive members of society.

When I think about confronting the PTF an uneasy shiver slithers through me and in that instant Logan's eyes briefly meet mine. He studies me carefully like he knows what I'm thinking, what I'm planning. His legs widen and he runs damp palms along his jeans before he turns the questions back to Nova.

"There has been no sign of them at all?"

"Nothing," she says, her long black hair flaring around her pretty, sun-kissed face as she gives an adamant shake of her head.

"Okay," Logan says and exhales a frustrated sigh before redirecting the conversation. "Did you get a good look at who did this?"

She nods. "The PTF."

Logan's fists clench and I can hear his blood rush faster, but he keeps himself in careful check, the way a good leader always does. But as Nova delivers the blow, confirming what I already suspected, I realize she's not telling Logan anything he doesn't already know either. Has her news brought back painful memories of the way the officers killed his parents years ago? Or does his worry stem from something else?

I watch his throat work as he swallows. "What happened to the others?"

Hands folded on her lap, Nova's gaze drops to the floor and there is real sadness on her face when she says, "Some didn't make it."

Logan closes his palm over hers. "And the others?"

"They fled." Her eyes widen, then turn hopeful as they lock back on Logan. "Maybe they went to Richmond's Village in the Jasper Mountains."

Logan's nod is slight, but his voice sounds unconvinced when he answers with, "Let's hope so."

Suddenly Nova's words sink into my brain, and as I digest what she's actually saying my pulse leaps. If there really are other compounds such as this one, then it's quite possible that someday we could reach one and all live normal lives.

Logan's next question catches me off guard and my heart stills as I wait for an answer. "Why didn't you go with them?"

I catch a moment of hesitation before she speaks and it's that hint of uncertainty that has me wondering if she's being completely truthful.

"I couldn't," she hurries out, her voice rising an octave. "They had me trapped."

Logan goes silent for a moment, and scrubs his hand over his chin. "Which brings me to my next question," he says quietly. "Why did they let you live?"

She shifts unnaturally on the sofa and I can tell she's uncomfortable and trying to hide it. Her eyes cast down in thought before she grips the hem of her sweater. With a quick tug, she pulls her shirt up to expose a deep purple scar near her hip. Collective gasps cut the silence because every wolf in the den knows there is only one thing that can cause such an ugly wound.

Silver.

"They shot me, and left me for dead. But lucky for me, the bullet only grazed my hip and I was able to gouge out the flesh around the wound before any of the poison could seep into my blood."

There is cold calculation in her gaze, but from the captivated looks on everyone's faces it's clear I'm the only one who sees it. It does, however, have me thinking more about the PTF. From what I know about them, they rarely miss their mark and always verify their kills. So why didn't they ensure she was dead?

When a tremble moves through her, Logan puts his arm around her shoulders. "Okay," he says, soothing her in a soft tone. "It's okay, Nova. Nothing is going to happen to you."

She makes a tortured noise, and that's when I see tears clinging to her dark lashes. "How...how do you know?" she asks, her voice trembling slightly.

Logan reacts to the fear in her and drags her closer. "Because you're with me now. And as long as you're with me, nothing is going to happen to you."

With that, she blinks the water from her eyes and gives him a big smile. Even though I know Nova is in need of comfort, and Logan is her alpha, the wolf in me doesn't like the way they're connecting, the way he is empathizing with her. I fight down the tightness in my throat, grab a pillow and plump it with my fists.

"There is something else," she announces.

I sit up straighter, eager to hear what else she has to say.

"Before they left I heard one guy talking on his cell phone." She pauses to give a shiver. "He said something about feral panthers."

Gem and I exchange a knowing look. Thanks to one panther, she managed to escape and make it to safety while the rest of her family was chased through the mountains. We know so very little about these shape-shifters, but one thing we do know is that they run purely on instinct and the human part of them lacks our sense of right and wrong. Which makes them a very dangerous enemy.

Then again, I can't forget about the one who let Gem go. So maybe they aren't all blood-thirsty monsters like we believe, and maybe if given the chance they can be taught control, and eventually live normal lives.

"And a few minutes later the men all took off," Nova adds, pulling my thoughts back. "I think they were going after them."

Logan gives a slow shake of his head, like he's piecing together the chain of events.

She delivers her next words slowly, as if to emphasize the importance of them. "I also heard them talking about a place called Lewis Lake."

Lewis Lake?

I search the recesses of my mind, trying to figure out why that name sounds so familiar to me. Was it a place where I'd once hunted and killed a deadly drug lord, or was it simply a geographical location taught to me by Miss Kara, the lady who educated my old master's enslaved wolves?

I'm not sure. But what I do know is that this whole situation feels off. There is something about Nova that I can't quite put my finger on. I don't know what it is, or what she's up to, if anything, but I definitely plan to find out.

3

As rain begins to patter on the roof of the den, I inch my eyes open and glance around the tight confines of the cabin. I have no idea what time it is, but judging from the angle of the near full moon as it briefly cuts through a heavy cloud to peek into our only window, I'd hazard a guess that it is well past midnight.

The air around me grows heavy, suffocating, and after experiencing freedom in the mountains, my wolf growls low, hating the claustrophobic feeling closing in on her.

Haunting memories of being held captive in my small cage come rushing back, and I quickly rise up from my crouched position on the hard floor. My body protests as I stretch my limbs and my joints pop and twist while I pad silently across the wooden slats.

My glance moves over Gem, Sandy and Nova who are all curled up on the mattress, to Logan and Stone who are both hunkered down and asleep near the door. I don't miss the fact that the sofa is empty, my father nowhere to be found.

Even though I know I should be sleeping, because something tells me I'm going to need my strength in the days to come, I step over Stone and hear Logan mumble something in his sleep. I still for a brief moment, then once I'm sure they've both settled back into a deep slumber, I pull on a pair of snow boots left by some previous tenant, twist the door open, and step outside.

The cool wind hits my face like a hard slap, pulling me wide awake, and big, heavy raindrops spill over my body and plaster my long, blonde curls to my head. I shiver as I blink a fat droplet from my eyelids and edge away from the den, not wanting to wake the others.

The heavy snow, now wet and slushy from the downpour, squishes beneath my oversized boots. Without conscious thought I wrap my arms around my body and hug my sweatshirt tight, all the while ignoring the fact that it's far from waterproof and the thick cotton is growing heavier by the minute.

Moving silently I walk to the edge of the cliff and glance down, taking note of the unnatural silence around me. Deep in the valley below the flames are all but gone, murky smoke polluting the air and obscuring the fire-ravaged village.

A branch cracks behind me, heralding someone's approach. Using slow careful movements I turn around and brace myself, my eyes peering into the inky night as I breathe deep to drag in the intruder's scent. That's when I spot him. A tall shadow emerging from the dark forest. My father's glance moves to mine, and he advances with purpose, the air around him awash with blood.

Fresh blood.

But it's not the blood from any animal I've ever encountered. This blood is foul. Rancid.

Diseased.

A strange sound gurgles in the back of my father's throat and when he moves closer I nearly gag from the sickly odor that comes with him. I catch a streak of crimson trickling down his chin before he quickly swipes it away.

He puts his bloodied hands behind his back as if to obscure them from my vision, but it's a failed attempt to hide them from my probing eyes.

"I take it you can't sleep either," he says.

Realizing he's trying to redirect my thoughts, I look past his shoulders and search the ground. But when my glance comes up empty, no dead carcasses in the near vicinity, I ask, "Are you hunting?"

"Deer. But it got away."

I give a dubious look and I'm about to press, but when he asks, "What now Pride?" my brain shifts focus.

For a moment silence hangs heavy as I turn my attention back to the destroyed village. A long while later I break the quiet.

"I can't stop thinking about what happened to Logan's family." As the fight for life and death plays out in my mind's eye, cold shivers move through me, twisting and knotting me up inside. "What if they're all..." My words fall off as guilt gnaws a hole in my gut.

"No one is blaming you," he says, as if he can hear the internal struggle going on inside my head.

Surprised by his insight, I jab my thumb into my chest and fight back the urge to yell my next words. "I'm blaming me."

"Why is it you think this is your fault, Pride? The PTF did what they've been trained to do. Seek and destroy."

I spin to face him. "What they've been trained to do is wrong." When he hesitates, and doesn't jump in and agree with my convictions, I wave my hand toward the valley below and this time there is nothing I can do to stop myself from shouting my response.

"What? You think this innocent pack deserved to be burned from their homes, or worse, burned to death?"

"No. But not all wolves are good, Pride. Just like not all humans are. I suspect there is no way for the PTF to know the difference."

My gaze darts to his and since he opened the door to this conversation, I decide it's time to grab hold of the knob and tear it clear off its hinges.

Holding no punches, and glaring at the man whose blood rushes through my veins, I say, "This insight comes from your own wolf experiences, I presume." Not only do I want to rip open the secrets between us, I want to toss them on the ground and stomp on them until they can no longer hurt me.

The truth is, when I made the decision to get to know my father, I knew it wasn't going to be easy. Lessons learned have taught me that *nothing* in this life is ever easy. But in order to face my future, I know I have to understand where I came from. In order to do that I have to confront my past, no matter how dark it is, or how much I might hate what I might discover. And right now, whether I like it or not, my traitorous father is the only connection I have to my heritage.

"Yes," he says honestly, his voice deathly quiet. "I know this from experience." He takes a small, tentative step toward me. "I've done things. Things I'm sorry for. Things I hope you'll one day forgive me for."

Anger hits with the force of a hurricane wind. "You say you left the compound to protect us, so the master couldn't use your empathy against us. Fine. I accept that. But that didn't stop you from harnessing other wolves and using them to do your killing."

"I didn't just leave that compound to protect you. I left so you'd never become like me."

"And by '*like you*' do you mean a traitor to your kind?"

"I got involved in things that weren't easy to get out"

I press my palms to my temples. "Then, why now? Why, after all these years did you decide to come back? That's the part I don't understand."

We exchange a long look, then he answers with, "Because it was time."

Frustrated by his cryptic answer, I spit out, "What is that supposed to mean?" My feet stomp in the slush and I hug my damp sweater to my chilled skin. "That's not even an answer." As I pace to the jagged edge of the cliff, I listen to the rain gush down the mountain's rock face and wonder what it is he's still not telling me.

He steps up beside me and glances at the sky. His eyes are distant, like he's remembering something from the past as rain soaks his face. "I never meant to hurt you, or your mother."

When I think about my mother, I gulp air, a tortured sound catching in my throat.

"I want the hurting to stop," I say around the lump lodged in my esophagus. I wave my hand toward the valley below. "I want all of this to stop."

We stay like that for a long time, both lost in our own thoughts, then my father finally breaks the quiet by saying, "I know there is nothing I can do or say to keep you from going back to California, but when you do, I need you to remember one thing."

I stare at him, and wait for him to elaborate. Once again silence ticks on for an endless moment until I finally say, "I'm listening."

"You can't ever forget what's in your nature, Pride. You can't ever forget that sometimes you have to let your wolf rule. It's the only way we can preserve our species."

I give a savage shake of my head, wanting to leave that part of my life behind me. "I'm not an assassin. Not anymore."

"I'm not suggesting you are."

"I just want to be free and live a normal life. That's why we all came here."

"Look Pride, what I'm trying to say is that there are two sides of you. I know you want to live a normal life, that of a typical teenage girl, but you can't ever forget the primal side of you. It's what makes you who you are and it's what keeps you alive."

I think about that side of me, the brutal wolf that killed on command. My stomach sours and I turn my back. "Not anymore."

"Don't be so sure. When the time comes, your wolf will know a split second before you do what needs to be done. You need to listen to her."

I spin back around and stare at him. When I realize what he's suggesting, I ask, "Are you implying that I should kill all the PTF? Wouldn't that simply confirm their theory that we're monsters?"

"All I'm saying is you have to know when to let the animal side rule and when to let the human side take control." His eyes cloud with something that resembles remorse and I wonder if that trace of regret is for things he's lost or things he's going to lose. "It's important. For your future. And the future of the pack."

While I don't really know what he's getting at, I do know that I'm not going to kill anyone. My hands are stained with enough blood as it is.

Exhausted, I turn back around, and when my glance lands on Logan, I stiffen, a gasp catching in my throat.

Exercising caution, he takes a step toward me. His face is drawn tight, his eyes feral. "You shouldn't be out here."

As he approaches, I take note of the quiet distrust in his eyes as he glares at my father—a reminder that my father once kept Logan caged in his underground prison. I understand the hatred and suspicion Logan feels toward the man who betrayed our trust, the trust of our kind, and in no way do I blame him for it.

While I chose to stand by my father, to get to know him, the choice wasn't made because I trust him. I don't. But everything in my gut tells me that he's the key to my past, which is the key to my future, and that I have something very important to learn from him, something only a father can teach.

I don't know what that something is, and it's quite possible that I'm wrong, but I'm not about to miss out on an opportunity to learn. Knowledge isn't only power, it's the fundamental answer to surviving in this new world.

Unease moves over Logan's face as he breathes deep, and I wonder if he's catching traces of that same fetid odor that assaulted my senses earlier. A moment later something in the alpha's expression changes, softens. He sucks in a sharp breath and it startles the nocturnal animals and sends them into hiding. Twigs snap and cut the silence as Logan and my father glare at one another.

"What?" I ask, my glance darting back and forth between the two.

Logan opens his mouth like he's about to speak, then something passes between the two, some unspoken message, some level of understanding that leaves me confused.

When Logan closes his mouth, my father relaxes slightly and turns to me. "Get some sleep, Pride. Tomorrow night's the full moon and we all need to be prepared." With that he disappears inside the den, leaving Logan and me outside. Logan steps up to me and his steady hands rake my wet hair back off my face as he assesses me.

"Are you okay?"

I want to ask what just happened between him and my father but when he uses the soft pad of his thumb to swipe the rain from my face my words lodge in my throat. His gentle touch combined with the deep concern in his eyes has my stomach clenching and my heart pounding hard against my ribcage.

"Come on," he whispers. I don't budge as he stands over me, looking so big, so strong. So male. A shiver of awareness awakens my wolf and it's all I can do to keep her leashed. "Your father is right. You need rest. We all do."

I look past his shoulder and when I think about going back inside the cabin I feel a moment of panic. "I don't want to go back in there." I stop and look skyward. "I want to be out here. It feels less..."

I pause, looking for the right word, but Logan comes to my rescue and says, "Confining."

"Yes, confining," I agree, thinking about how astute he is and how well he can read me, even without a mental connection.

"Okay, come on." He captures my hand in his and guides me to the den where he uses the wooden overhang to keep the rain from reaching us. With my back pressed against the exterior wall, he inches toward me and his close proximity pulls a shiver from deep within. Feeling suddenly breathless, I lick a raindrop from my lip as my glance moves over his face.

His eyes drop to my mouth and for a minute I think he's going to kiss me. Goosebumps break out on my flesh when he grips the hem of my drenched sweatshirt. I don't miss the hunger in his touch when he rubs the wet material between his fingers. It's that raw ache of need in his eyes that has me remembering the gentle way he once explored every inch of me, the intimate way he cared for my body that night in the cave.

Intense blue eyes examine my face and he pushes against me, transferring warmth between our damp bodies.

"Take this off," he says, his voice low, throaty as he pulls my sweater from my waist.

The soft pad of his thumb scrapes over my trembling skin and as his heat reaches out to me, his warm breath chases the chill from my body. My pulse pounds at the base of my neck and a deep primitive sound rises from the depths of my throat as my wolf reacts to his primal essence and animalistic scent.

"Logan," I manage to push past my lips.

He inches back and I immediately miss his heat. But when he begins to peel his raincoat from his shoulders, I realize he has mistaken my shiver for something else.

He clears his throat, his lips hovering close but never touching mine. "You're soaked and you need to get out of these clothes and into something dry."

My hand touches his face. "Logan," I begin, not really sure what I'm going to say. Not really sure what I'm asking of him, or even if I have the right to ask it.

His big palm closes over my hand, his eyes searching mine, seeking answers. "Pride," he says and I don't miss the emotions clouding his stormy blues when he continues with, "You know I love you. You know I'm going to fight to the death for you, don't you?"

I instantly think about that night at the compound. When I found out about my father's betrayal and took comfort in Stone's arms.

"Logan...I..." A look passes between us and everything in his expression tells me he knows what I'm thinking, what I've done, and what I'm trying to say.

"Shh," he whispers as he helps me from my sweater. "It's okay."

"I didn't mean..." My words die on my lips as I stand before him with my body and heart exposed. Even though

I'm still half dressed, I've never felt so naked. So vulnerable. "I never meant..."

He puts his coat over my shoulders and looks at me long and hard before saying, "It's okay."

I stare at him, dumbfounded. "You're going to forgive me? Just like that?"

Logan sinks to the ground and pulls me down with him. "Yes."

"Why?"

"Because sometimes love is about forgiveness, Pride."

I swallow, the air between us charging as his warm eyes move to my mouth, yet he still doesn't kiss me. Instead he pulls me toward him until my head is settled on his chest. He holds me tight, and I think about how his hands are full of strength and power, yet capable of such gentleness when he touches me. I snuggle in closer, his body so achingly familiar to mine that I can't help but take comfort in his warm strength.

We stay like that for a long time, and listen to the night sounds around us. Trees creak in the downpour, animals scurry about and I can almost feel the brush of wind when off in the distance a bird of prey takes flight.

My mind shifts to what my father said to me, and how he hopes that one day I can forgive him. Finally I break the quiet and say, "Logan."

"Yeah?"

"I don't really know anything about forgiveness."

"You will. Soon enough."

There is an edge to his voice, one that has unease scraping along every vertebra in my spine. "What makes you say that?" I lean back until our eyes meet.

"Call it gut instinct," he says but I get the sense that he might know something I don't. With that he pulls me back until I'm once again snuggled against him. As he rakes his hands through my hair, I drag his scent into my lungs. The clean, earthy fragrance of his skin combined with the possessive way he holds me makes me feel so warm and safe. It also makes me think of the way he cared for Nova.

"Logan," I begin again.

"Yeah?"

"Did Nova's behavior seem a little strange to you?"

"How so?"

"I don't know." I pinch my lips together in thought and curl the hem of his t-shirt around my index finger. "I got this odd vibe from her. Like there was more going on than she was saying."

"She's just been through a lot."

"I know but..." I pause, and struggle to choose the right words so I don't come off sounding like a jealous mate.

While I work to formulate my thoughts, he says, "She's not strong like you, Pride."

I tilt my head to see him and don't miss the unfettered pride in his eyes when they meet mine. My heart misses a beat and it takes effort to speak.

"Are you sure that's all it is?"

He gives a slow, confident nod. "I'm sure," he answers. "I've known her my whole life and I think she's suffering from shock and trauma."

I think about it for a moment longer and come to the conclusion that Logan must be right. Maybe, under these horrific circumstances, Nova's behavior is completely normal. After all, I really don't know what normal is in this outside world. And maybe there is nothing more going on than my wolf reacting to another fertile female.

I blink, straining to keep my eyes open, but my lids are so heavy, weighted from the strain of the day, that I can't fight the pull of nature any longer. I close them and drift in and out of consciousness for hours, floating on some level between sleep and awake, until a flock of chirping birds pull me from my slumber. My lids flutter open as the brightness of a new day greets me.

The morning air is crisp, but I don't feel the bite in the wind as Logan's heat continues to wrap around me, protecting me from the harsh, mountain elements. I rub the sleep from my eyes and emotions pool in my heart as Logan stirs awake, his lips turning up at the corners when his glance lands on mine.

"Good morning," he says. "Sleep okay?"

I nod and while I listen to the steady flow of his blood, my thoughts turn to his missing family, and I can't help but worry about their safety. I also think about our safety, the future of our kind, and what I must do if I want us all to live normal lives.

My eyes meet his but from the way he looks at me I get the sense he already knows what I'm about to say. "You know I have to go back, don't you?"

"I know."

"You're not going to try to stop me are you?"

"No."

Deep inside my wolf bristles, because she knows this could very well be the most important fight of her life. While she's courageous in the face of danger, she also knows how badly it could all end.

"I'm going to leave after the full moon tonight."

I take a moment to strategize, to put together a plan of action. As I think about how to bait the monsters, the cruel predators who need to be stopped from killing innocent wolves, Logan's voice pulses around me and pulls me back.

"Just so you know, I'm coming with you."

"So am I."

I turn to see Nova standing by the open cabin door, but when my glance clashes with hers, and I see black bleakness glittering beneath her pale blue eyes, darkness churns inside me and I swallow uneasily.

If we're all backtracking in a bold attempt to bait the hunters, why then, do I get the feeling that I'm the one walking into a trap?

4

Fortunately, the night of the full moon passes us by without incident. Thanks to Logan and all he taught me about survival, I am now better able to control my wolf when she's at her most vulnerable.

Late last evening and well into early morning, the seven of us all kept a careful watch over each other while we chased game through the mountains, sating our primal hunger and satisfying our wolves until the next lunar pull.

As the sun slowly creeps over the mountain peaks to light the new day, I silently rise up from my sleeping position on the hard wood floor, and scurry backward until my shoulders are pressed against the cold cabin wall. A familiar chill that I can't seem to shake moves through me as the spruce boards chafing my back suck the heat from my bones.

I wrap my arms around myself and pull the stale cabin air into my constricted lungs. I scan the room and try not to feel so confined after a blissful night of running in the wide open mountain space.

I blink against the thin veil of light slicing the dark cabin, and peruse my contented pack. In a mass of arms and legs, their bodies are snuggled together as they sleep in the small den, collapsed in a heap of exhaustion after a long, hard night. Deep inside my wolf howls in delight as she appraises her new family, elated to finally be free from the master's prison. When I think of my master and his control over the old compound, however, a shiver runs through me, because I never, ever want to feel powerless like that again.

But then a darker thought hits, one that reminds me Logan's missing family might not be so lucky. I swallow, and my heart pounds a little faster in my chest when I think about going back, to fight this long overdue battle with the PTF.

I'm not naïve enough to believe it's going to be an easy fight, or that I'll walk away unscathed. In fact, I understand that I might not walk away at all. But I can't let that debilitate me. Others are counting on me, and I've come too far to back down now.

"*Hey.*"

The sound of Stone's voice inside my head, greeting me with such warmth and emotion, draws my attention. Looking rumpled and sleepy, his dark hair is a tangled mess as he sits up and shimmies backward until he's pressed against the wall beside me. With my senses tuned, I take in the tousled state of the powerful alpha inching closer.

There is something about his familiar scent and disheveled appearance that reminds me of when he was a pup, and all the times we used to play together in the nursery. Then my brain fast forwards to the present, and the kiss we recently shared in his cell.

He stretches his long, muscular legs out, and my skin tingles in awareness as this boy—my true mate—shifts even closer until our thighs are scraping. The gentle familiarity of his touch doesn't feel wrong, but it doesn't feel right either. At least not after the intimacies I shared with Logan.

"*Hey*," I finally say back as I think about the secret he kept from me for so long. But I now know he kept me in the dark about our bond, about our true destiny, because he was simply trying to protect me.

I angle my head and his eyes are warm when they meet mine, and for a minute I feel like I can't breathe. So much has happened between us, so many truths have been revealed, ones that have me wondering what could have been—what very well might have been—under different circumstances. But I know now is not the time to be thinking about connections and mates, not when we're about to face the biggest fight of our lives.

"*Stone.*"

"*Yeah?*"

My mind rewinds to what Nova told us the first night we arrived. "*Did the name Lewis Lake sound familiar to you?*"

His brow furrows and he rubs his chin. After a long thoughtful moment, he slides me a look and gives a slow shake of his head. "*No. Why?*"

"*I don't know.*" I shrug one shoulder and feel his warm knuckles brush against my hand. I swallow as he reaches out to me both physically and emotionally, and I have to force myself to keep my mind on the current crisis. "*I have this strange feeling that I've heard it before. I just can't quite figure out why.*"

He looks down, like he's searching his memory. Then I feel him move deeper into my thoughts before I can stop him. When he exhales a long slow breath, I know he's tapped into my private worries.

"*I don't trust her either, Pride,*" he says. We both shoot a glance toward Nova, who looks completely content snuggled up next to her pack's alpha.

"*You don't?*" I hurry out, a chill scurrying up my spine. When his glance darts back to mine, the distrust I see in his eyes mirrors my own, giving credence to my concerns about Nova's motives. "*I thought it was only me who felt that way.*"

I take a moment to consider Logan, and can't discount the fact that he knows Nova better than Stone and I do. But can he be so caught up in his own grief, his own worry for his pack's safety, that he's failing to see beneath her surface? Or am I really making an issue out of nothing at all? My wolf merely threatened by another female?

"*Logan doesn't think I have anything to worry about.*"

At the mention of Logan's name, Stone's eyes darken to a deadly shade of black and his nostrils flare. He rakes his hair from his face, only for it to fall forward again.

His jaw tightens and I brace myself because I know what's coming next. "*You don't have to go back you know,*" he says.

I look away from him, anger erupting inside me. "Yes, I do." I say the words out loud as I cut the mental connection between us.

"Pride—"

"Haven't we lost enough, already?" I ask, trying to keep my voice from rising to the point of hysteria as the others begin to stir around us. "Our childhood, our parents, our freedom?"

I glance back at him in time to see silver shards bleed into his black pupils. "We could end up losing more," he warns.

My stomach rebels when I see the raw, tortured look on his face, his worry hitting like a fist to my gut. I suck in a hurried breath and it's all I can do to inflate my lungs.

"And we could end up winning," I counter, sounding more breathless than I would have liked. "Either way, you know we have to try. I'm not about to walk away from Logan's family. They're missing because of me, Stone." I wave my finger back and forth between the thin column of space between our bodies. "Because of us."

The air between us charges, a volatile eruption of emotion

that neither of us can keep in check. I'm sure anyone within a fifty mile radius can feel it, and if we don't get it under control it will surely trigger a reaction from the wolves around us. Stone fists his hands, his predatory glance going from me, to Logan, back to me again.

"Logan never should have let you go back to the compound. You were finally safe. He should have ensured you stayed that way. It only proves that he can't take care of you the way I can, Pride."

When I sense his mounting fury, I work to keep my own anger in check and try to reason with him, but as I do it simply reminds me that he's been imprisoned his whole life and is reacting the only way he knows how.

"First," I say in a calm voice that belies my emotions, "It wasn't Logan's choice to go back, it was mine. And I wasn't safe, Stone, inside the compound or out. What happened here proves that." I wave my hands around. "I could have been a part of all this. None of us will ever be safe until we stop the PTF." I lower my voice, and add, "Besides, did you really think I'd leave you there, to suffer at the hands of the master while I ran around free?" I give a slow shake of my head. "Maybe you don't know me so well, after all."

"You're wrong, Pride. I know you better than anyone knows you, maybe even better than you know yourself." He goes quiet for a long time, then his voice is dark, grief-stricken, and completely possessive when he finally says, "I let you walk away from me once. But you came back and now that we're together again, I won't be able to let you do it a second time." He exhales slowly and adds, "I can't."

When I hear the need in his voice, a storm rolls through me and my gut clenches. "Stone, please. Don't."

"I can't, Pride." He gives a slow shake of his head. His hair falls forward to mask his eyes, but it does nothing to hide his emotions when he says, "I won't be able to make it through it. Not again."

His grief penetrates my heart as he pulls his legs up to rest his elbows on his knees. Without conscious thought I reach over and brush the hair away from his eyes. But when I do, a deeper emotion that he can no longer hide from me moves over his face.

His hand closes over mine to still it, and his palm is warm against mine as he holds me tight. "I don't want you to go back, Pride. I don't want anything to happen to you."

I blow a wayward lock off my face, and with more bravado than I feel I announce, "Nothing will happen to me."

There is desperation in his voice, a level of anxiety I've never heard from him before when he counters with, "You can't say that."

"I'm going back," I say firmly, then sit quietly, my lips pinched tight as I give him time to let that settle in his brain.

He grits his teeth and the laugh lines playing along his mouth deepen—not that his life has given him much to laugh about.

I can feel his blood run cold when he says, "Then I'm coming with you."

We sit there for a long time, lost in thoughts while we stare at each other. Heat radiates from his hand to mine, but I still can't shake the coldness inside me. Then, a distant voice breaks the moment and has my thoughts jolting back to the present.

"Pride?"

My head jerks up to see Logan staring at me. He rises to his full height, and drives his hands into his pockets, pulling his pants low on his hips. Watching his hands has me thinking of my own and I instantly pull away from Stone's protective hold and hurry to my feet.

"Everything okay?" he asks, his voice full of dark suspicion as he zeroes in on Stone.

Dry gobs of cotton clog my throat and it forces me to push the words past my lips. "Everything is fine," I manage to get out as I move toward the sink for a drink. I draw a shaky breath and continue with, "Stone was just telling me he is coming with us."

I walk past Logan, and my primal side bristles as his warm earthy scent, one that reminds me of clean morning air and fragrant pine needles, wraps around me. I know it's an instinctive reaction, my female wolf responding to the boy she once mated with because the waning moon is still affecting her.

Logan and Stone glare at one another for longer than what's comfortable, then Logan looks at me as the wolves around him begin to stir. The concern brimming in his blue eyes touches a soft spot deep inside me and forces me to look for a distraction. I swallow my water in big gulps and it helps me get myself under control.

Logan steps toward me and his voice is low when he says, "We're all coming with you, Pride. I thought you understood that."

"No," I blurt out, not wanting anyone else to get hurt because of me. "It's not a good idea."

I spin back around and when I see the respect and strength in his eyes as they lock on mine it reminds me that these wolves—ones who live so differently from what I'm used to—are pack animals, ones who live and die together. Unlike most of the wolves I've been imprisoned with my entire life, this family takes care of each other, and will do what it takes to keep *all* members of the group safe.

I give a hard shake of my head. "Sandy's in no shape and Gem has been through enough."

Sandy and Gem both look at me in confusion and I try

not to flinch under their probing gazes. Gem speaks first. "Pride, we're family now and where I come from, family sticks together. You didn't leave me back at the compound and I'm not about to leave you now."

Sandy blinks from her perch on the bed. "If it wasn't for you..." she begins then swallows before saying, "I don't know what would have become of me. This is as much my fight as it is yours, Pride."

The fact that I now have a family, and they're determined to fight this battle with me, has my heart doing a little flip in my chest. It also reminds me that these shifters believe in me and it's their faith that has me renewing my vow to find Malcolm and the others and end this fight with the PTF once and for all.

"Then we'd better get a move on it," I say around the lump forming in my throat, knowing now is not the time for a public display of emotions. It's time to concentrate on the mission ahead, and strategize our best move. "We're wasting precious daylight hours."

With that everyone climbs to their feet and we all begin the final preparations for the long trek back. We travel down the mountain, and less than an hour later, fake identification in hand, my father returns with a vehicle, a massive SUV that can carry more than all seven of us.

While Stone shares a seat with Gem and Sandy, Logan rides shotgun. Nova takes the second last row and I climb into the far back, needing time with my thoughts as my father negotiates the car down the highway, toward the ferry that will take us back into the United States.

Retreating into myself, I stare blankly out the window, my mind working through the various scenarios that we might come up against. I look at the maps my father bought while he was in town renting our vehicle, and think more about Lewis Lake. I pinpoint the area on the chart, and while I'm sure I've never physically been to this specific location, I still can't shake the haunting feeling that I've heard of it before. I search my mind again, the answer continuing to dance out of reach.

But soon enough Nova is pouncing into the back with me, her silky hair pulled off her face, a long braid dangling down her back in a fashion that has me thinking of Ms. Kara.

I listen to the rapid beat of her heart and the elevated thud of her pulse. Her blood is running faster through her veins now, a hurried rush that she can't hide from me. Without saying a word she moves in beside me, and as I turn from her and glare out the window, I can feel her pale eyes drilling into the back of my head.

"Pride," she finally says when she realizes I'm waiting for her to make the first move.

Leaving the scenic imagery behind, I look at her pretty face and while I want to believe Logan, believe that she is suffering from trauma, my hackles bristle, and a dark shiver pulses in my blood. Warning bells clang in my head, because beneath her perfectly fabricated façade I catch a hint of something so foul it leaves a bitter taste in my mouth. As my stomach sours in response, every nerve ending in my body, every instinct I possess stands on high alert.

"Yes?" I ask as she turns those shrewd pale eyes on me.

"Do you have a plan?"

"Yes," I lie. Even if I did, I'm not about to let her in on it.

Her hand squeezes my arm, and I flinch at the contact. "It's very brave of you."

"What's brave of me?" I glare at her and wonder where she's going with this.

"To go after the PTF." She stops to give a mock shiver, her hand closing over the wound they left on her hip. After a good show of fear, she says, "I was lucky to get out alive." She pauses, then adds, "But from what I've heard about you..."

Her voice falls off and even though I feel like I'm walking into a trap, I ask, "What have you heard?"

"That you're a fearless warrior, Pride," she answers with bright eyed enthusiasm, her white teeth flashing in a smile. "A courageous leader."

Instincts sharp, my wolf gives a low menacing growl, her distrust evident in the way she reacts to the girl beside me. I continue to wonder what Nova is up to, and don't miss the fact that she's trying to bolster my ego. What I don't know is why.

"What makes you say that?" I ask instead of telling her the truth—that I'm just a girl trying to right a wrong and find her place in this strange new world.

"I guess if anyone can change the minds of the PTF it's you." She waves her hand, then tucks a wayward strand of hair behind her ear. When a small frown forms on her forehead, I study her expression and try to figure out what's really going on inside that head of hers. "It makes me wonder why we're all tagging along."

"I never asked you to come along."

Her smile fades and I feel her mood turn sober, dark. "Then again," she continues on as if I hadn't even spoken, "it's not like we could stay back in the village. Not after you led..." She stops midsentence, and gives me a sheepish look. "Well, you know."

I stare at her long and hard, my heart pounding in my ears as her words hit with the sting of a cruel master's whip. She goes quiet, like she's giving me time to absorb and digest what she's saying. But no one knows better than I do that it was me who led the PTF back there, and I'm responsible for the death of her family, the destruction of her entire village. I exhale a ragged breath and the tortured sound serrates the quiet of the SUV.

Nova leans into me, and my wolf stirs uneasily. Long

lashes shade her eyes and in a low voice meant for my ears only she says, "I guess that's why you want to fix this mess. I'd feel pretty guilty, too."

My chest tightens, and as anxiety gnaws at my stomach, I steel myself, hating that she's right about my feelings, and hating more that she can so easily read them. I work to slow my pulse and keep my blood flowing steadily, my instincts warning that the less she knows about me the better.

Nova squares her shoulders and levels me with a stare before gesturing with a nod toward the front of the vehicle. "We might be travelling with two powerful alphas, but if I were in your shoes, I'd be sure to take the lead on this mission. You know, so no one else ends up getting hurt."

As her words settle like a cold, chaotic lump in my stomach, I pull her scent deep into my lungs and despite my best efforts to keep my pulse steady, it kicks up a notch.

I move past the floral aroma on her tanned skin, the heady perfume of her natural wolf, and when I do I get the sense of something very dark beneath the fragrant mask.

Something very dark indeed.

5

After a long, uneventful ferry ride, and an even longer night of driving along the Pacific Coast highway we're finally well on our way to reaching our destination. From the back of the vehicle, I try to spend my time thinking and resting, understanding sleep might be hard to come by in the next few days, but when the SUV hits a bump in the road it pulls me wide awake.

With a new day upon us, I give up on sleep and blink my eyes wide open. I tilt my head to face the sun and as I drink in its mid-morning warmth, I let it seep under my skin, hoping it will chase away the chill in my body, one, as of late, I simply can't seem to shake.

I crack my window and the crisp autumn wind whips at my face and blows my wild, tousled curls into my eyes. Breathing deep, I tuck my hair behind my ears and inflate my lungs until my chest is fully expanded. While the sharp intake fuels my blood cells and helps pull me wider awake, it still doesn't keep me from craving a hot cup of coffee, the hazelnut kind like Mica, the elderly housekeeper who always tried to see to my needs, used to sneak me.

Off in the distance I catch hints of salty brine in the air and when the vehicle rounds the corner and I glimpse the Pacific Ocean just over the embankment, my heart begins to race.

As it pounds rapidly inside my chest, it makes me feel lightheaded, but that doesn't stop me from sticking my head out the window so I can listen to the liquid surf crash against the rocky shore.

As I take in the glorious sight—one that has always reminded me of freedom—my mind races back to the time when I shared secrets with Logan. I think about that special night I opened up to him, the night we talked honestly about our feelings and I told him what the Pacific Ocean means to me.

Without conscious thought, my glance darts to the front of the SUV, my wolf seeking the boy she once mated with. When I catch a pair of unguarded eyes staring back at me from the rearview mirror, it produces a familiar fullness in my chest, one that has my wolf howling from within. Logan's smile is slow, the warmth in his ocean blue eyes every bit as warm as the Pacific waters lapping nearby. But it's the hint of vulnerability I see shimmering below the surface that tells me he's thinking about that night every bit as much as I am.

We exchange a long, thoughtful look, the bond we share evident in the way our eyes connect. But as I think about the promise he once made to me, I realize so much has changed since the full moon we spent in the cave.

We've all been through so much, seen too much for wolves our age, and I can't deny that I no longer feel like the young, naïve girl who ran through the woods with a powerful alpha—a boy who taught me to hunt, feed. Survive. One who assured me that someday, when our fight is over, he'd take me to the ocean to play in the sand and surf.

But as I think about the war we're about to face, and

think about the things my father said to me outside the mountain den, I can't shake the uneasy feeling that our fight for freedom will never be over. Before I can stop it, a low groan rumbles in my throat and draws Nova's attention. I turn from her probing eyes and diligently try to dismiss the frightening thoughts, refusing to let my mind travel down that dark, dead-end path.

A movement in the seat directly in front of me gains my attention. I glance at Stone and when I feel him surfing the outer edges of my thoughts, I mentally push back. Our gazes lock and his haunted eyes search mine for answers, ones I simply don't have.

As emotions crowd me, I tear my eyes away to stare out the window, returning my focus to the mission ahead. I think about what we could face at Lewis Lake, I wonder if the two alphas—boys who are so completely different from one another—will be able to work together when the time comes.

Or will their hate and distrust for one another end in bloodshed?

That thought has bile pushing into my throat. When my father announces from the front seat that in a few hours we'll be approaching our destination, I harden myself, and get my mind back into the game of life and death.

We stop at a roadside gas station to fuel our vehicle as well as our stomachs. The master used to think an empty stomach made me a better hunter, which is the main reason I want my wolf full before trekking into the unknown. I don't want hunger pangs distracting her, and can't take the risk that an empty stomach will drive her to do something I might regret later. At least if I'm full, I'll be better able to keep her settled and focused on our pursuit.

After swallowing down half a tuna sandwich, the rich creamy mayonnaise thick and delicious on my tongue, I pop the cap on my can of soda. I take a huge gulp of the syrupy drink and stretch out my stiff legs as I make my way across the wide expanse of black asphalt toward the empty SUV.

From behind me a loud yelp pierces the air. I don't need to turn back to know it's the cry of an agitated German Shepherd. The heavy metal chain clanking along the ground fills me with horrific memories of my own collar as the dog bolts forward only to get yanked back inside the mechanic's bay beside the convenience store.

"We'll be gone in a minute," I whisper under my breath, understanding the animal is threatened by the motley crew of wolves who've trespassed on its territory, and is reacting the only way it knows how.

Not at all different from a boy I know.

When the mechanic yells at the dog and hauls him inside, I turn my attention to the fat, ginger colored cat scurrying out from beneath a camper. It cuts across my path, stopping long enough to hiss at me. With its fur standing on end, the cat arches its back in a defensive mode, a failed attempt to make itself look bigger and frighten the big bad wolf away. Unable to help myself, I bare my fangs, and when it runs across the busy parking lot and disappears under a set of wooden steps, my wolf howls in juvenile delight, eager to take chase.

Except I don't let her. Because the sight of the cat reminds me I have more serious matters at hand. Like the deadly panthers that have been unleashed into the world. A fine shiver moves through me as I take a moment to wonder what will become of them, and of the humans they encounter. Then I once again think about the one panther that gave Gem her freedom, one that went against nature, against its family. The same way some wolves go against their nature, and turn their back on their packs to live rogue lives—the way my father had.

With that last thought tossing the sandwich around in

my stomach and pushing a thick clump of wet bread into my throat, I swallow hard, and shade the sun from my eyes. I nurse the soda and strive to wash away the bitter taste lining the inside of my mouth and I catalogue our surroundings to get my bearings. That's when my father steps up to me.

Around a mouthful of mustard-covered hot dog he says, "I've been looking over the coordinates, and Lewis Lake is well off the grid. I don't think we should go in until after dark."

I think about that for a moment. It won't give us an advantage if we're up against feral panthers, but it could mean the difference between life and death if we stumble upon PTF officers. I'm well aware that all hunters are equipped with night vision goggles, but our night vision comes naturally, so the advantage is still ours.

"Okay," I agree.

He gulps down the last of his food, and wipes his mouth with the back of his hand before turning his full focus on me. Dark eyes move over my face, assessing me. "What do you expect to find there, Pride?"

"I don't know, but since it's our only lead I think it's the crucial first step in figuring out where Malcolm and the others are."

"Are you prepared to do what you have to if you come across task force hunters?"

"I'm prepared to talk, to reason with them. To show them we're not monsters."

His brows collide as his forehead creases. "How do you expect to do that?"

"By not killing them," I announce.

"And you think they'll let you live, just because you spare their lives?" I open my mouth to speak, but he cuts me off and says, "They're dangerous men and this is what they've been trained to do. It's all they know and they enjoy it, Pride. It's what they live for."

I tilt my chin, but don't miss the knot tightening in my stomach. "I changed the mind of one, didn't I?" As the words spill from my mouth, I wonder exactly who it is I'm trying to convince. Him or me. Either way, Logan's family is missing, and while I have no idea what is waiting for us at Lewis Lake, I know it's not in my nature to tuck tail and run in the other direction.

Expression wary, my father pinches the bridge of his nose, his battle-scarred face twisting in pain. I stare at him and my stomach sours in confusion.

Before I can ask what's going on, he says, "Let me ask you one thing." He pauses for a moment, and when he sees that he has my full attention, he asks, "What if you can't change the minds of many? What if this is a war that you can't win?"

When I catch scent of his apprehension, old fears creep into my thoughts but I quickly shove them out. "I can, and I will," I answer. I wave toward the rest of our pack who are still inside the convenience store. "I promised them all freedom, the chance to live normal lives outside the compound, and I plan on making that happen."

Signaling my disinterest in carrying on with this conversation, because I can't let his doubts cloud my focus, I perch on the passenger seat and turn my thoughts to the maps sprawled out on the dashboard. I run my finger along the highlighted path Logan has outlined and remember his stake in all this. He has a family to find.

"Define normal, Pride?"

My father's somber voice cuts through my thoughts like a silver blade, and my head jerks up with a start.

"What?" I ask.

"Define normal," he says again.

As I stare at him, he mops at a bead of sweat on his forehead and there is something so profound, so darkly disturbing in his eyes when he looks past my shoulder to stare at the long, black stretch of highway ahead of us, that it steals the words from my lips.

A warm afternoon breeze whips my hair around my face, and when my father exhales slowly I catch a foul scent in the wind. I can't pinpoint the root of the odor, but I do know it's the same tainted stench that assaulted my senses when I spotted my father emerging from the woods two nights ago.

Looking more tired than he did this morning, he circles the car and climbs into the driver's seat beside me. As he slowly drums his fingers on the dashboard, a fine shiver moves through me and my hackles spike. My wolf begins pacing, howling to break free and run. Even though she doesn't recognize the putrid scent clogging the cab of the vehicle, she doesn't like it, doesn't like that it makes her feel restless, edgy.

Fearful.

I'm glad for the distraction when the others begin to file out of the convenience store and walk toward us. When I catch Logan's glance, Nova keeping pace beside him, he cocks his head to the side. His eyes are questioning, distrustful, worried beyond his young years when he sees my father sitting in the vehicle so close to me, which begs the question, what does Logan know about my father that I don't?

As I mull that concern over for a moment longer, and think about our private conversation outside the den the other night—when Logan assured me I'd soon learn about forgiveness—my mind races with questions, mainly, why aren't we all past the point of keeping secrets?

"We should go," I say more to myself than anyone else, and while I want to question Logan, to determine if he's keeping something from me, I know now is neither the time nor place, especially considering the way Nova continues to cling to him.

With that we all pile back into the vehicle. By the time we reach our final destination and pull the SUV off the road to take a path into a remote area of the woods, the last ribbon of light fades from the sky.

As darkness descends over the forest, we cut a bumpy path through the threadbare trees, and drive until the dirt road narrows in on us. Once the vehicle stops Nova slides the door open and I climb out behind her. I stand still for a long moment and listen to the night sounds. In the far distance, I hear the familiar echo of a cannon sounding its last blast of the night, frightening off any remaining birds from a local vineyard. A trickle of unease shivers through my bloodstream.

We're close, I realize. Far too close to my former prison for comfort, which once again has me wondering why the name Lewis Lake strikes me as familiar.

I wrack my brain and search the recesses of my mind but my thoughts shift when my glance lands on Sandy. I feel a moment of worry for her and can't help but wish the young girl was better insulated from all this danger. Since she's carrying a child, she should have been taken to safety before this mission, but I do know that she's right. She has lost as much as I have in this senseless fight, maybe even more so, and needs to be a part of the battle to end the war on wolves every bit as much as I do.

I take a moment to compose myself. Then, in my quest for information, I step over a fallen tree and pull the scents of the forest into my lungs. Moving deeper into the dark woods, I can feel the sky-scraping trees closing in on me from all angles, the canopy of leaves making it that much more challenging to search for signs of danger.

With my pack at my back assessing the situation, I continue forward. Dry autumn leaves, crisp and colored from the changing season, crunch beneath the soles of my over-sized boots.

Animals scurry about, weaving their way around the trees, and birds take flight as we intrude upon their domain. With the instinctive knowledge that we could be walking head first into danger, I still for a moment, every nerve in my body on high alert.

Even though my wolf is fearless, eager to right wrongs, she knows better than to jump into any situation without a plan of attack. But since I don't know what we're going to find out here in the middle of nowhere, I'm unable to detail an outline, unable to strategize the best course of action.

Needing to know what we're up against, what sort of monsters will emerge from the deadly darkness encroaching upon us, I hunker low and rub dry leaves between my hands, my wolf feeding off the aroma of the forest.

I scan the area and search the ground for tracks, a hunting trick Logan taught me while we chased game in Olympic Park. Squishing the leaves in my hand until they crumble, I bring them to my and inhale. I let the various scents seep into my bloodstream, and when I catch a distinctive smell, one that warns of death and danger, I jackknife to my feet and let loose a low, distressed howl.

"What is it?" Stone asks, his eyes piercing the darkness around us as he steps up to me. His gaze searches mine and I can feel him trying to read my thoughts. "Panther?"

I shake my head and brush the decaying leaves from my hands. As they fall to the ground in a shimmer of color, I answer with, "No, but a female wolf has been through here recently, and she's frightened."

Stone scents the woods and spins around in a circle to commit our current location to memory. His voice is calm but I don't miss the underlying urgency when he says, "We need to move. Fast."

I nod in agreement and with that he gestures for the others to follow. Using hurried footsteps, I fall in behind him and while he takes the lead on this trek, Logan stays at the back of the pack, keeping every one of us in his sight at all times.

Our feet fall mutely as we track deeper into the woods, until the sounds of the highway, the ocean, and all forms of human life are left far behind.

My skin begins to itch, burning in warning, and I resist the urge to claw at my flesh as I continue to scan the forest. I angle my head to the side, sorting, searching, listening for signs of danger.

I take another step, but when Stone stops abruptly, I crash into him. My nose smashes into his hard back and I let loose an undignified oomph as my legs falter.

He spins on the balls of his feet, and in a movement so fast it catches me by surprise, he curls protective arms around my waist and pulls me against him. His familiar scent drowns out the smells of the forest around me, and practically steals the breath from my lungs. I open my mouth to speak, but he presses a finger to my lips to silence me.

"*Sorry*," he whispers into my thoughts, as the rough pad of his thumb scrapes across my bottom lip. His touch, warm and deliberately intimate, sends sensations rippling through me. A flurry of emotions passes over his face, and everything in the hungry way he's looking at me, purposely dragging his thumb over my mouth in a slow agonizing caress, confuses my wolf and tortures my soul. "*I didn't mean to hurt you.*"

"I'm...I'm okay," I say, but he doesn't make a move to let me go. Instead, his nostrils flare and heavy lashes briefly fall over his dark eyes as he sends me a look, one that promises so much. We stay like that a moment longer, my body completely immobile as he keeps me anchored to his.

Somewhere in the near distance, a twig snaps, the sharp sound piercing the quiet and dragging me back to reality.

"*What is it, Stone?*" I finally ask breaking the moment between us. I look past his shoulders, trying to see what spooked him as hurried footsteps herald the approach of the others.

Logan moves close and fixes Stone with a dangerous look, but the alpha with his arms circled around my body still seems reluctant to break his hold. Stone glares back, but when I push on his arms, he uncoils them from around my waist. After I extricate myself from his grip, my father steps up beside us all and when he gestures to a spot behind Stone, I use that time to pull myself together.

"What's going on?" Logan asks between clenched teeth, tension crackling in the air.

Stone aims his finger, and using our exceptional night vision, we all look in the direction he's pointing. Collective gasps can be heard when we glimpse an old cabin camouflaged beneath a cluster of weeping trees. Tucked far off the beaten path, the place is invisible to the road, the sky, or even hikers. And for some reason that has the hairs on my nape tingling.

As I stare at it, and recall the scent saturating the fallen leaves, my mind takes me in a bleak direction, one that has me realizing how a wolf's tortured screams would go unanswered way out here in the middle of nowhere.

That dark, disturbing thought has a shiver moving through me and I don't miss the strange tingling in my bloodstream. I will the image from my head but there is nothing I can do to stop the tremble running along my spine.

As if sensing my distress Logan steps close, his stance protective, and his eyes are full of genuine concern as his body hovers over mine.

"What is it, Pride?" he asked, his comforting heat wrapping around me like a tight glove.

"I don't know." My hackles spike and I shoot Logan a weary glance. "Something isn't right."

Logan places his hand on the small of my back, but I quickly sever the intimacy, unable to take comfort in his affectionate contact because I need my wolf sharp, focused fully on this mission and not on how nice it is to be touched by him.

Logan's voice is a coarse rasp when he says, "Maybe we should go back."

Wind hums around me and the fine hairs tracking along my spine stand on edge, but my wolf isn't about to turn back now, isn't about to surrender even if I want to.

Which I don't.

I'm driven by a need to find the pack of wolves who once stood behind me, a pack that could very well be dead because they fearlessly crawled into my personal hell without fully understanding the consequences.

With that last thought urging me on, I take a few more steps and brace my hands on a decaying log as I carefully climb over it. Insects scurry about beneath my palms, and the pungent scent of wet moss reaches up to greet my nostrils as I glance up to see Stone inching forward. He looks back to check on me and the darkening of his eyes as he scans for hidden enemies and possible threats makes me strangely uneasy.

Nova moves in beside me, her breath coming in hurried gulps as she whispers, "Do you think Malcolm and the others are inside?"

I watch her for a minute and don't miss the urgency in her eyes. Her blood is pounding hard, rushing faster than a wolf on the prowl, and I wonder what's elevating her heartbeat— anticipation? Or fear?

"There is only one way to find out," I answer.

"You're going in?" she asks, one perfectly sculpted eyebrow arching inquisitively.

I'm about to answer, but Stone waves us forward and we all push past the low hanging branches and step up to the pitch black cabin. I sniff the air, and when a breeze washes over my face, the deadly stench of sulphur and silver thickens my throat.

"PTF," Logan says coming up beside me. Pewter punctures the blue in his eyes as he scans the tree line. "They're nearby." He sweeps his hands through his hair to push it off his face and says, "It's not safe here, Pride."

My heart begins to beat faster because I know we can't run away. Not yet. Not without first checking to see if Malcolm and the others are caged inside. Besides, even if I'm suddenly feeling ill prepared, isn't facing the PTF part of my pursuit? I just wish I was facing them on my grounds, and not theirs.

I stalk closer to the cabin and try to scent the inside. When my efforts prove futile, I turn to Logan. "Do you—?" I begin to ask.

"I can't tell. The place is locked up tight."

I go up on my tip toes to peek inside. It's dark, and I can't detect any movement, but that doesn't mean it's empty.

When my wolf growls, Logan moves closer, his body caging me between the cabin and his chest. "What do you see?" he whispers.

"Nothing, and that's the problem. I have to get inside."

"Pride—" he begins.

Just then Nova comes up from behind, looking wind-blown and nervous, her eyes wide, and her blood is rushing so fast I fear her heart is about to explode.

"I found a small window around back. It's open," she hurries out and there is an intensity about her that makes my feral wolf want to crawl out of my throat and snap at her. Her glance fixes on me. "It's tiny. Only big enough for you to fit through, Pride."

I narrow my eyes and peer at her. "Did you see anything inside?"

"It looks like a small bedroom, and it's empty."

"Okay," I say, and work to strategize my next move, but when Stone joins us and his anger hovers like a dark rain cloud, it pulls my focus.

Wild eyes lock on mine, and an untamed sound gurgles in the back of his throat before he says, "You're not going through it, Pride. I'll break down the door first before I let you go in there alone."

My pulse thrums harder in my throat and I fight to steady it. "You can't," I whisper, then draw a fueling breath, pulling the scent of the deadly hunters into my lungs as I look at the shifters surrounding me. They're homeless because of me and I know I can't let them down. "The noise will draw the attention of the PTF and I don't want to face them until I free the others."

"What if it's a trap?" Stone points out, pitching his voice low to match mine.

"What if it's not," I counter, intent on finding out who or what's inside, and if I don't find the others, I at least hope to find information leading to them. "The PTF aren't aware that we know about this place." As I address his worries, I can't help but think about Nova and the darkness I feel in her. But the truth is we've come too far to back down now.

My glance lands on my father, and I find him standing guard over Gem and Sandy. His face is tight, his body on high alert, but there is a new weariness about him, one I've never seen before. I'm intelligent enough to know there is something going on with him. While I feel it in every fiber of my being, I know now is not the time for questions. Now is the time for action.

"Logan?" I say, looking at him.

A guttural sound rises from the depths of his throat and it's clear he doesn't like what I'm about to do, but he also knows it's our only choice and nothing he does or says is going to stop me.

His warm palm cups my face. "The first sign of danger, you get yourself out," he warns, and I give a quick nod. I'm about to move, but he captures my elbow and holds me for a moment. He gives an encouraging squeeze, and as he communicates silently with me, showing his belief in me, it fills me with bravado. "I've got your back, okay."

"You have got to be kidding me?" Stone barks out, his voice rising in the sudden updraft rushing through the forest.

I put my hand to his chest to calm him. "Stone, it's okay. I'll get in and get to the front door as fast as I can and let the rest of you in."

"It's not okay," he bites back. "You might not be able to make it to the front door."

"I know what I'm doing."

"Are you sure, Pride?" he asks, his back ramrod straight, his eyes drilling into me. "Are you sure you know what you're doing?" As we glare at each other in strained silence, the air around us charges with volatile electricity, and I know in an instant what he's really asking.

Before I can answer him, he changes tactics and I feel his voice inside my head, his words for my ears only. "*You said yourself you didn't trust Nova. What if she's up to something? What if she led us here on purpose?*"

I think about that for a minute and the longer I consider it the more ludicrous it begins to sound. Nova is just a young girl, one who has been completely sheltered from life's harsh realities. I steal a sideways glance at Logan. With a frown on his face, his hands are fisted as he watches the silent exchange between destined mates. I can't forget that Nova is a part of his pack, and she must want to find her missing family every bit as much as he does.

"Maybe we're way off base, Stone. Maybe Logan is right and we have nothing to worry about."

At the mention of Logan, Stone turns to stare at him and their gazes clash in a silent struggle.

The muscles along Logan's jaw clench and there is real danger in his voice when he says, "I'm not going to let anything happen to her, Stone."

Stone's mood blackens and he gives a humorless bark of laughter. "Yeah, because you've been doing such a good job of that now, haven't you? You don't know how to take care of her, Logan. Not like I do."

When they move toward one another, I press a palm to both their chests and try to defuse the situation before it escalates and gains the attention of hunters. There is a frantic edge to my voice when I say, "You two can stay out here and fight it out if you like, but I'm going in."

With that I turn from them, and their voices fall off as I disappear from their line of sight. When I spot the small window, barely big enough for me to crawl through I take a deep breath to fuel my courage. I go up on my toes and inch the glass all the way open and still for a moment, listening for movement inside.

Stale air spills outside and I nearly choke on the bitter taste. I grip the window frame and hoist myself up on the sill until my knees are balanced on the rigid casing. I peer into the darkened room, committing every nook and groove in the tight space to memory as I slip my legs through the opening and shimmy forward until I'm halfway inside, then I drop to the floor, and brace myself.

Keeping deathly still, I glance around the cold, dank

room, and using slow, careful movements I drop to my knees to look under the unmade bed, the headboard jammed against the wall beside me. After finding the space empty, I push to my feet and take one small step, determined to get to the front door to let the others inside.

The wood floor board groans beneath me, and I stop mid stride and hold my breath. I stay like that for a long time, but when I hear no sounds in response, no guns cocking, or the pounding of feet coming my way, I step around the mattress and move toward the closed door leading to the main room.

I listen for sounds outside, and can feel Stone trying to enter my thoughts. "*I'm okay*," I say, and to ease his worries I let him hover on the outer edges of my mind as I quietly push open the door. Exercising caution, I slip into the next room and the second I do, my senses are assaulted with the coppery tang of death and my stomach revolts in protest.

Blood. Danger. A violence so brutal that it puts my former master's cruelties to shame, swarms around me in a kaleidoscopic burst. Bile punches into my throat and when my knees falter, I grip the door handle to balance myself.

Knowing bad things have happened here, and in fact could still be happening here, I work to keep my emotions in check, work not to vomit as the bitter scent of brutality drowns out all the other smells in the small cabin.

Breathing through my mouth, I can almost feel the coldness of death seeping into my bones. I push forward and pad quietly toward the front door, but when a frightened whimper catches my attention, I spin in the direction of the sound. Dread takes hold because deep in the darkened shadows I spot an intruder. Tall. Powerful.

Armed.

When eyes as deadly as silver glare at me, survival instincts kick in and my wolf turns feral. Sharp canines puncture my gums, and as the figure emerges from the semi darkness, I turn and face him straight on. Except, I quickly realize, he's not the intruder.

I am.

My nostrils flare and I suck in a quick, fuelling breath. The rush of oxygen in my bloodstream parts the fog clouding my rattled thoughts, and allows me to think with more clarity. A shudder moves through me because for the first time since we set out on this dangerous journey the tumblers all begin to fall into place, and I know at once why Lewis Lake sounds familiar.

But more importantly I know there is a traitor amongst us.

6

In the darkened cabin, I take a split second to size up my opponent, to determine what I'm up against and figure out the best course of action.

A sliver of moonlight filters in through the small window and highlights a path across the cabin. As the light plays with my imagination and creates monstrous shadows on the walls, I can almost feel them closing in on me, taunting my wolf and encouraging her to rip clear of her restraints. I work to fill my lungs as icy shards of fear shoot through me, a violent, instinctive storm that urges me to shift.

Kill.

As that one word pounds through my head, I make a deep guttural sound and my wolf tears at my flesh, frothing, clawing, fighting to rip her way from my body. Howling, and in kill or be killed mode, I know my control is about to snap, my wolf about to take action.

Moments before she emerges and goes for the man's throat, I call on every ounce of strength I have to stop her, because from somewhere down deep, another thought registers, warning me not to let her off her leash. Despite what my father told me, that sometimes we need to let our wolf rule, I know if I do I'll never be able to prove we're not soulless monsters.

I draw a quick breath and marshal my wolf into submission, being careful not to make any sudden movements in the process. As she hunkers low and whimpers from down deep, I keep motionless, my eyes trained on the dangerous hunter dwarfing me.

From my peripheral vision, I take in my surroundings, understanding I'm smack dab in the middle of a PTF safe house—a wolf caught in the lion's den—and what I do next could help end the war on our kind, or forever put us at risk.

I use all my senses to assess the dangers before me, my mind working to defuse the situation so I can make this man understand who we are and want we want. But when my glance meets a set of dark, dangerous eyes, ones that are drilling into me with wild suspicion, I feel a seed of doubt, some small part of me warning that I just might be fooling myself, that this is a battle I can't possibly win.

Refusing to let that stop me—unable to let that stop me—I open my mouth to speak, but my words die an abrupt death when the man stalks closer, his hard face coming into full view, and I don't miss the way those black eyes of his move over my face with careful regard.

A hunter sizing up its prey.

My wolf wails again, urging me to let her free but then suddenly the ruthless face glaring down at me softens around the edges, his expression morphing into something that resembles relief. Bewildered by this turn of events I pull in his scent. I catch hints of anxiety, but I get the strangest sensation that his nervousness isn't because of me.

It's for me.

As my pulse thrums in my throat I watch his posture change, and that's when it hits me. I know who he is. I almost breathe a sigh of relief, but the small whimpering girl caged in the corner triggers alarm bells in my brain and warns me this hunter is no longer on my side.

Instinctively, fight or flight instincts kick in, and I widen my stance. Prepare.

"Easy there, Pride," he warns, and I hear something desperate in his voice, something I wouldn't expect from a PTF officer. He lifts one hand in the air, his large palm facing out in surrender while the other hand hovers over the gun slumbering in his holster.

While I know he's packing silver and the odds are not in my favor, I know they're not in his either. I bend my knees and maintain a combative stance while I work to keep my voice level.

"What's going on?" I ask, and don't dare take my eyes off him as the girl begins to whimper louder, her frightened cries echoing off the cabin's bare walls.

Emotions gather in a knot inside my stomach, but I know better than to shift my focus and try to help her. I'm smart enough to know that I can't afford to get distracted and any sudden movements on my part could be misinterpreted by this trained hunter and force him to reach for his gun. He might have spared my life once, but I have no reason to believe he'll do it a second time.

"It's not what you think." he says with a frown, his disturbed glance flickering between me and the small metal cage.

As my mind visualizes the torture being carried out in this cabin, there is nothing I can do to keep my talons from elongating or my lips from peeling back to expose sharp canines. As my wolf zeroes in on the man's jugular, one I've punctured before in a dirty alley way when a trio of hunters failed to slow me with their poison, I listen to the rapid flow of blood in his veins.

"We don't have lot of time and you need to listen to me. You have to let me explain."

The scent of his concern mingles with the girl's fear. The fetid aroma saturates the room and there is nothing I can do to keep my wolf from feeding off the medley of emotions. As she pulls the tang into her lungs it makes it that much more difficult for me to keep her harnessed.

I watch the way his pulse jackhammers in his neck when he says, "I know what you're thinking."

I touch my tongue to the tip of a sharp canine. "If you knew what I was thinking, you probably would have drawn your gun already."

His dark eyes study me and his voice is deceptively mild when he says, "I know you're not a killer, Pride and you need to let me explain." But beneath that calm façade I know he's every bit as leery of me as I am of him.

He lowers his hands in a show of trust and as I watch him with suspicious eyes, studying his every move, I find nothing calculating in his actions, nothing to suggest he wants to hurt me.

My hackles settle, but my wolf stays on high alert, her guard firmly in place. Silver bullets or not, there is no way she is about to back down in the face of this hunter, not when there is a young, frightened shifter locked in a cage beside me.

While my wolf is ruled by instincts, I'm smart enough to know I need to listen to what he has to say before making my next move, so I quiet my heartbeat and offer him the chance to speak.

"Explain," I say facing him straight on, my primal side angry and unafraid.

As I settle my thoughts, I can feel Stone inside my head, surfing around and sorting through the images in my mind, but before I can stop him, before I can tell him I have every-

thing under control, the sound of the window smashing penetrates the quiet inside the cabin.

My eyes snap up and briefly connect with the officer's
before we both turn in the direction of the sound. My heart
lurches as the hunter draws his gun and takes aim at the
boy/wolf about to attack.

In a fierce possessive rage, Stone shifts mid air and dives
for the man's throat. The officer peels off a shot, but it goes
wayward and lodges in the ceiling as Stone pins him beneath
his big, beefy paws. Stone presses down on the man's chest
and the weight of the wolf forces the gun from the hunter's
hands.

Ruled by his primal side, Stone's roar echoes in the still-
ness of the black night, and his large, deadly canines flash in
the thin column of moonlight as animal bloodlust
takes over.

"Stone, no!" I cry out, but there is nothing I can do to
calm him, nothing I can do to stop the feral wolf bent on his
own agenda.

Fear propels me forward and I let loose a loud howl as I
prepare to pounce, but Logan steps in front of me to shield
me from danger. Looking hard and dangerous as shards of
silver bleed into a storm of blue within his eyes, I gulp air and
wonder if he, too, is going to go wild on me. But when I look
at him, really consider the boys standing over me, I see him
for what he is. Strong. Steady.

In complete control of his wolf.

"Don't go near him, Pride," he warns. "Not when he's
like this."

With that, Logan tears off his clothes and shifts. Despite
having just warned me, he flies through the air, his beautiful
streamlined body catching lift before he clamps down on the
back of Stone's neck. An explosion of violence erupts in my
ears as he gives a savage shake of his head. Stone yelps, his

jaws unhinging as the powerful alpha tears him clear off the hunter's body.

Panting hard, the officer lets loose a cry and scrambles backward. He swipes the blood from his neck and reaches for his gun, but even in the middle of a deadly battle Logan has enough foresight to kick it my way before the officer can grab it. It scuttles across the wood floor, out of my reach.

As the situation goes from bad to worse, my glance locks with the officer's, and I know our thoughts are running in the same direction. We both dive for the gun at the same time, but I manage to reach it seconds before he does. He lands with a hard thud, and I quickly tuck the weapon into the back of my jeans then grab hold of his shoulders to drag him away before he gets caught in the crossfire.

With my breath coming in ragged bursts, I turn my attention to the two alphas. While neither is packing silver, they're both packing deadly fangs, and even though we have regenerative abilities, there is no way a wolf can come back from a torn and shredded jugular.

In an untamed fight that could end in death, Logan and Stone roll across the floor, and the fresh scent of blood fills the air as they rip into each other's flesh. Frantic, and knowing I need to neutralize the situation before one of them ends up dead, I give the officer a deadly glare.

"When I'm done with these two, you have some explaining to do," I warn between gritted teeth, then pull the gun from my waistband.

I hold it over my head, but the officer jumps me, his large palm wrapping around my wrist. As he shackles my arm, I call on all my wolf strength and prepare to break free from his death grip.

I jerk away, but when he says, "Don't, they'll hear it," my brain comes to a screeching halt.

As I digest his words, my eyes study him and when I see

real worry lingering in the depths of his gaze, I understand what he's saying, what he's warning me about. It also becomes glaringly apparent that if he was really working against me, he surely would have let me fire and signal his team.

Taking that as a good sign, I announce, "They already heard one shot." A shiver moves through me as I look out the smashed window and listen for signs of his comrades' approach.

The two wolves crash against the cabin wall and the floor below me shakes violently. Blood smears on the wooden slats, and I have no idea how this fight will end, because while both wolves know each other's strengths they also know each other's weaknesses.

The man gives a fast shake of his head and the action draws my attention. "One shot lets them know someone is out here, two shots will give away our location."

As I think about that a loud, painful yelp stabs through my thoughts, and I know things have gotten completely out of hand. I turn the gun over in my palm, and consider my next move. If a second shot brings the officers, could this be the opportunity I've been waiting for? The opportunity to reason with them.

"Don't," he says, impatience sharpening his words. He narrows his eyes and when he sucks in a sharp breath, I realize he knows what I'm thinking. In a low warning voice, he says, "Don't take on more than you can chew, kid. You're not prepared."

Before I can explain what I'm trying to accomplish, my father comes bursting through the front door. Wood splinters and hinges twist as he tears his way into the cabin. The sound echoes in the night and while a single gunshot might not give away our bearings, I realize the noise of a crashing door surely will.

The look on my father's face is terrifying, and when I

glance past his shoulders to see Gem and Sandy huddled beneath a tree, Gem trying to soothe a stricken Sandy while Nova runs away like a scalded cat, I realize how desperate things have become. I tuck the gun back inside my waistband for safe keeping and turn my attention to my father.

"Enough," he bellows, the bite in his command stopping the other wolves cold. He walks up to them, and grabs both alphas by the scruffs of their necks. They snarl back as his angry glance goes from Stone to Logan back to Stone again and his voice lacks any sort of tolerance for their antics when he says, "Shift."

A second later both boys return to their human form, and as they pull their clothes back on, my father's glance takes in the girl caged in the corner before he turns his focus to the officer braced against the wall.

"What's going on here? What is this place?" he asks. I remain hunkered beside the officer, my wolf ready to pounce should he make one wrong move against my father. While I don't want to kill him, and ruin everything I'm trying to prove, I'm not about to let anyone hurt those I call family.

Not ever again.

"It's a PTF playground," he answers quickly, fully aware that what he says next could very well mean the difference between life and death for him. "They hunt for sport," he adds, and juts his chin toward the young girl in the cage. "But I'm not part of this. Ask Pride." As I process what he's saying, the truth of what goes on in this place hits like a sucker punch. My breath escapes my lungs in a hiss as I think about this man's warning.

"Don't take on more than you can chew."

Suddenly his words begin to resonate with me, a reminder that these men are monsters—cruel, ruthless humans who enjoy the hunt. As I consider that a moment longer, I suddenly feel foolish for coming here unprepared. In my quest to be more human I tamped down my wolf instincts when they were warning me of danger—warning me about Nova. A cold chill rushes through my bones, because while I know we're all still alive, I also know things could have gone down a whole different way.

The officer's voice drops an octave, the seriousness of his next question apparent in his tone. "What you really should be asking is, how do *you* know about this place?"

My father's jaw clenches, and he angles his head to look outside. I follow his gaze and when he spots Gem and Sandy, Nova nowhere in the near vicinity, understanding lights a fire in his shrewd eyes. He turns back to the crouching officer, flecks of pewter glinting angrily in his eyes, and his body braces for battle.

"You'd better start explaining."

The officer shakes his head and looks at the busted door dangling on one twisted hinge. When it swings wildly in the wind and cracks against the doorframe we all tense. The hunter carefully climbs to his feet and with his body on edge, his eyes fill with something that resembles unease as he glances at some distant spot in the woods.

"There's no time. We have to get out of here."

I breathe deep and my ears perk, listening for the sound of an approaching task force. Taking me by surprise, my father grabs a fistful of the man's collar and picks him up off the floor. The man's legs dangle beneath him, and I see my father's sheer strength, that of a full grown wolf, long into his power.

He bares sharp fangs in warning and wets his bottom lip as he zeroes in on the man's throat, a reminder to the officer that he could end his life before his next heartbeat.

"If I find out this is a trap and that you're leading us somewhere you'll wish I had killed you here and now," he warns. "Because, believe me, if you're working against us your death will be slow and painful. You have my word on that." I reach up and touch my father's arm and when I do his muscles bunch beneath my fingers. His back straightens and he adds, "If it wasn't for my daughter, you'd be dead already."

With that he lets the man go and in a heap of exhaustion, my father drops down beside me. I look closer and note the deepening of the lines around his eyes. That's when I see how much that burst of energy, a show of former power, cost him.

The girl whimpers, and my stomach revolts when I look at her, the sight of her stuffed in that small cage tormenting my soul and enraging my wolf. Remaining in a crouched position I move away for the others. On my hands and knees I crawl across the scarred and dented floor, talking slowly, calmly, in the same soothing manner Logan once used with Nova.

"It's okay. I'm not going to hurt you. No one is going to hurt you anymore."

She sniffs, her big brown eyes watching me timidly, unsure, terrified.

Anger, fear, but mainly disgust creeps into my tone when I think about the men—these so called humans—that did this to her.

"Are you hurt?" I ask.

She wipes her nose with the back of her hand and gives a quick shake of her head. But then her nervous glance flutters to the officer.

I narrow my eyes, my throat tight with emotions. "Did he hurt you?"

"No," she says softly and when she speaks I realize how young she is. Where is her family? Her pack? "It...it was others like him," she whispers, and by others I know she means PTF officers.

I grab the lock to examine it and feel a burst of red as

anger ambushes me. After a quick tug I realize it's going to take a lot more strength than I have to break it.

"What's your name?"

"Blaze," she answers in a voice so low I have to strain to hear it.

"Hang tight, Blaze," I say softly. "I'm going to get you out of here."

I look around for something to jimmy the lock with, but Logan crawls in beside me and with one quick yank he tears the bolt clear from the metal cage.

An invisible band squeezes my heart as we exchange a private look, but no words need to be said for him to know what I'm thinking, what I'm feeling.

Eyes guarded and uncertain, the girl crawls from the cage, and the second she's free from her tiny prison Logan and I help her to her feet. When her knees falter, her legs not quite steady after being confined for so long, Logan slips his arm around her waist to support her.

I turn to see the others, but when I search for Stone and my glance comes up empty, my heart lurches, blind panic filling me. When it occurs with dawning horror where he's gone and what he's about to do, air leaves my lungs in a rush. Despite what Nova did, despite how she set me up to die at the hands of the PTF, I don't want Stone hunting her. I don't want to be responsible for any more deaths than I already am.

A loud howl full of distress crawls out of my throat and I rip at my shirt, needing in the most desperate way to find him before the hunters catch him in their crosshairs. If he comes up against one, I know what will happen.

I know what he'll do.

Returning to fight mode, my canines sharpen and some-where in the distance I hear the others yelling at me, their voices echoing ominously in my head. Pain shivers through my nerves and I ignore their protests as my bones prepare to shift and slide into place.

"Pride, no," Logan says, and it occurs to me that I've never seen his face so serious, never heard his voice so harsh when speaking to me.

As I drop to all fours, eager to shift, he moves in front of me to block my path and when I give a savage shake of my head, a warning that he's not to stand in my way, I can hear the officer and my father exchanging dire words.

I turn to glare at them and that's when the officer looks at me pointedly and challenges with an unwavering stare, "If you go, you won't make it back. These aren't the kind of men you can reason with."

"He's right, Pride," my father says darting an anxious glance my way. "We need to get out of here. Now."

When the full weight of their words cut through the chaos in my brain, panic invades my stomach and my pulse skyrockets.

"I can't leave Stone out there. He's in kill or be killed mode." While I know he's smart, I also know his survival instincts are strong, and he'll do whatever it takes to survive.

Whatever it takes to protect me.

And that could very well lead to his death.

The officer doesn't even try to soften the blow when he announces, "Then he's as good as dead already. And there isn't anything you can do to help him."

As a fresh wave of silence envelops the cabin, my heart beats faster, confusion and anger hitting at the same time. Do they really think I'm going to leave Stone to his own fate?

With my stomach twisting and churning, my mind races, refusing to turn my back on the boy who would die for me. My wolf prepares, orchestrating her next move, because she knows what we have to do, and she knows I'm not about to let anyone stop me.

"I'll go," Logan says, his eyes glistening pewter fire as they meet mine. Before I can even digest what he's saying, he's moving with purpose. Using predatory precision, he pounces out the door and a moment later he's airborne. Without breaking stride, he leaves a pile of clothes in his wake, his body shifting and morphing into a powerful, streamlined wolf.

"Meet me at the vehicle," is the last thing he says before he completes his shift and gets swallowed by the dark, dangerous night.

1

After hurrying back to the vehicle, everyone climbs inside, but I'm too antsy, too frantic to sit still. With a pile of clothes in my hands, I pace the dark forest, my ears perked for sound, my wolf ready to take chase should she need to.

I scour the dark woods and worry about Logan and Stone's safety. There is nothing I can do to keep my anxious mind from conjuring up deadly scenarios, dangerous situations the two could easily find themselves in. As I fret and my imagination kicks into high gear, I hear the SUV door click open.

"It's okay, Pride," my father says in a hushed voice as he steps up to me. "Logan knows what he's doing."

Even though I know Logan is a powerful, skilled alpha, one who knows his way around the woods, my father's words still fail to comfort me.

I flick him a glance. "Stone doesn't. He's reacting."

While I know it's not his fault, that he's only doing what he believes he has to, I also know if he's going to survive out here, he has to start evolving, adapting to the way things are done in the outside world.

Over the last month, Logan taught me all about survival, and after tonight I realize it's now my turn to step up and teach Stone. Before he gets himself killed. Before he proves to the PTF that we really are bloodthirsty beasts ruled only by our survival instincts.

In the far distance a shot rings out and the little bit of food I have left in my stomach clumps together to form a heavy ball. Anxious and on edge, I wring Logan's shirt with my fists and while I listen to the bullet whisper through the wind, I also listen for the sound of a fallen wolf.

"I should have gone after him." My feet crunch dead leaves as I hug the pile of clothes to my chest, and when I spot a rabbit dart into the underbrush, it's all I can do to keep my agitated wolf from taking chase.

I catch another sound in the near vicinity, and I brace myself, my ears perked as both my father and I stop to listen. With our wolves on guard, prepared to attack, I scent the forest, pushing past the pine, moss and moist earth as I peer into the thick woods.

When I hear branches move and leaves rustle, I growl and hunker low. A moment later, when two very distinctive scents hit at the same time, I nearly sob with relief. I sprint to my feet and the second I spot the battle worn wolves emerging from the dark, I rush to them.

They step into the clearing and I hurry forward to examine them for injuries. A breeze flutters their thick coats and the chill in my bones runs so deep that when they both brush up against me, I take a quick moment to soak in the warmth of their fur.

Logan is the first to shift and we exchange a look as I hand him his clothes. He dresses and I turn my attention to

Stone. The second I see a sticky layer of blood coating his thick fur, I gasp, and wonder if it's his or Nova's.

"Stone?" I ask, my eyes moving over his face as I feel a quick flash of panic.

"He got caught in a thorn bush," Logan says, answering my unasked question.

I glance at Logan. "And Nova?"

Logan turns away from me, like he can't bear to meet my eyes when he says, "She's gone."

I swallow. "Gone?"

"She got away," he clarifies as Stone morphs and stands to his full height, his angry eyes softening when they land on me.

I hand Stone his clothes and when another gunshot rings out, deep in the forest, I cringe. Instinctively, the alpha wolf steps closer to me, as if to shield me from the danger.

I blink up at him and feel a measure of panic. "Do you think...?"

When he gives an uncertain shrug, I turn to Logan. He jams his hands into his pockets, and my eyes track the deep scars on his chest, scars inflicted by my former master. Scars inflicted because of me.

"Logan?"

I don't miss the hitch in his voice when he says, "I'm not sure we'll ever know."

I think about the girl he grew up with and know none of this can be easy on him. "Logan, I'm sorry."

He looks at me, his nostrils flaring and I see real sadness in his eyes. He almost feels a little distant when he says, "I'm the one who's sorry, Pride."

"We need to move," Stone announces, breaking the moment as he brushes up against me to pass, his knuckles scraping along my body in such a familiar way.

When I feel his tension, I turn to him and while I know he's hurting, I ask the question anyway, "Are you okay?"

He nods and continues toward the SUV. He growls at the officer sitting in the front passenger seat before climbing into the far back of the vehicle to sit next to me.

Once we're all inside, Stone's hand closes over mine, his touch conveying without words what he's feeling, what he needs. My pulse races and I don't say anything in return. Instead, I let him hold me and breathe in his anxiety as I listen to his heart pound in his chest.

Staring out the side window, I watch the black pavement fly by and when I think about how badly things could have gone down, how close I came to losing the boy clutching my hand like it's his lifeline, I try not to cry.

With my breath coming in shallow pants and my body trembling almost uncontrollably, I look for a distraction, something, anything to keep me from breaking down in front of the others. Knowing I need to be strong for them, I turn my attention to the vehicles zinging by on the highway and focus on the hum of the wheels as my father negotiates the SUV along the winding road.

I have no idea where we're going, or where he's taking us, but I can't seem to ask, can't seem to get the words past the knot in my throat.

After a half hour of driving, he pulls the vehicle off the side of the road, slams on the brakes, and shoves the gear shift into park. The turn is so abrupt, I jostle to the side and fall against Stone, and he squeezes my hand in reassurance.

"What's going on?" I ask, and try to figure out why my father suddenly stopped in the middle of nowhere.

I watch him exchange a deadly look with both Logan and Stone in the rearview mirror, and when the scent of his rage pollutes the interior of the vehicle, my wolf yelps. Stone's eyes darken to a dangerous shade of silver as my father climbs from the SUV, crosses in front of it, and practically tears the passenger door clear off its hinges.

The officer, as if expecting this turn of events, puts his hands up palms out. "Okay, okay," he says, the panic he's feeling apparent in his tone. "Take it easy. I said I'd tell you everything I know."

He slides from the seat. When my father slams the door with a resounding thud, I bolt forward and climb over Gem, Sandy and Blaze as they watch the action unfold. Fearing he's about to assassinate the man out here where his body will never be found, I jump from the vehicle.

Without looking behind me I know both Stone and Logan are tight on my heels. Loose gravel crunches beneath my boots as I hurry toward the trees fringing the highway.

Leaving the vehicle on the side of the road, keys still in the ignition, my father backs the officer up until they're shrouded by foliage.

Once he has him in the shadows, he says, "We're not going any farther, not until you answer my questions."

With a common goal in mind, Logan and Stone instinctively begin to work together. They flank the officer while my father proceeds with a pat-down. When he finds no tracking devices, or a second gun, he stands up and folds his arms across his chest.

"First," he says, a new hardness in his tone as his lips peel back. As I watch him, I can feel my own gums tighten in response. "Who are you?"

I don't miss the worry in the officer's voice when he answers with, "The name is Mike Sanford."

"Okay, Sanford, you say you're not involved, why then, were you in a PTF hideout with a caged wolf?"

"Call off your dogs first." he says, his nervous glance going back and forth between Stone and Logan. "Then I'll tell you everything."

My father's laugh is humorless as he pins him with a glare. "I don't think you're in any position to be making demands."

"Listen—"

"No, you listen. You spared my daughter's life, which is the only reason you're still alive, but if I find out you're part of the team hunting for sport, those two," he says, stopping to nod toward the deadly shifters baring their fangs, "are going to make sure you disappear."

"I'm not part of the team. I'm not a part of any team." He looks at me before adding, "Not anymore."

I step up to him and tilt my chin until our eyes meet. "What do you mean, not anymore?"

"I know you're not a monster, Pride. You opened my eyes to that." He stops to rake shaky hands through his short hair. "Which is why I assembled a new team after our encounter at the Canadian border. But when headquarters found out, they made a visit to our branch. I tried to explain to them that not all wolves are bloodthirsty animals and that perhaps we needed to change tactics."

"And?"

"And they determined that I was growing soft. They disassembled my team and kicked me off the force."

A shiver turns my blood to ice and when I exhale, my breath fogs in front of my face. "You're working alone then?"

"I'm working alone, but it's not what you think."

"Tell me what I think."

"Let me just tell you what I know." He pauses, but when I say nothing he continues. "I went there to stop them from killing that girl. You were the last person I expected to find in the safe house."

"I never expected to find you there either."

He looks confused for a moment then asks, "How did you find out about the hideout, anyway?"

I think about Nova and the ugly bullet wound that didn't kill her. I realize it had all been for show. That the officers had let her live so she could deliver me to them. I keep this to myself. Sanford doesn't need to know, not yet, maybe not ever, of Nova's deception.

"Why did they want me?" I ask, speaking over the loud hum of the cars flying by on the freeway.

His brow furrows, and his laugh is rough, almost maniacal, as it serrates the night and curls around me. "Think about it, Pride. You're the one who got away. And no one ever gets away."

"So they wanted to hunt me then? For sport?"

"Yes."

"And they forced Nova to lead me to them?"

"She wasn't forced," Stone says, his angry voice raking down my spine like a jagged-edged knife.

My gaze jerks to his and I can tell he's in fight mode. "What are you talking about?"

"She wanted you out of the way."

As I consider that possibility, my glance goes to Logan, and I watch his chest rise and fall while he fists his hands at his sides until his knuckles whiten.

I stare at him for a moment and when the pieces fall into place my vision goes a little fuzzy around the edges. It takes effort to speak when I say, "You were supposed to be her mate."

"It wasn't like that between us," he answers through clenched teeth.

"Maybe someone should have told that to her." Rage erupts inside me when I think about the senselessness of all this. None of this should have happened and now Nova is out there all alone, and we have no idea if she's dead or alive.

I think about the caged girl, and jerk my thumb toward the SUV. "Who is she?"

He shakes his head. "I don't know."

"Why would they hunt someone so young?"

"A wolf is a wolf in their eyes. Age doesn't matter, and the young ones are usually more afraid and they feed off that."

"Do you have any idea who she is?" I ask Logan, wondering if he might recognize her from any of the packs he knows. Perhaps she comes from Richmond's Village in the Jasper Mountains Nova once mentioned.

When he shakes his head no, I wonder where her family is, or if she could have spent her life imprisoned by a cruel drug lord, like Stone, Sandy and me.

I turn to my father, "Do you think she's—"

"It's possible."

That has me thinking about my last conversation with the officer, when he assured me they were going to search the known drug lord compounds. "Has anything been done about the imprisoned wolves?"

"Yes, but not by us."

Unease crawls along my flesh and I wrap my arms around myself. "Panthers?"

He nods. "We can track them, but they're not so easy to kill."

"That's because they're cats and they have nine lives," Logan elaborates. "Their regenerative abilities are quicker than ours, and silver doesn't kill them."

"Nine bullets will do the trick, but they usually get away before you can pump all nine in. They're fast, Pride."

"We're faster and stronger," Stone announces, and I don't miss the way he angles his head to see Logan before he adds, "And there isn't an animal out there that can survive a ripped jugular."

As I think about wolves versus panthers, I swallow and push the next words past my lips. "We had a pack of wolves with us when we escaped from the compound. They were ambushed, and ran, but have yet to show up. Do you know if they're——?"

"We don't have them. We never did."

"Then there's a chance they're still out there."

"Maybe," he says, a brief hint of skepticism flashing in his eyes. "But if they are, I can help you find them."

"How?"

"I still have all my equipment, including my radio transponder."

Since I'm not a girl who trusts easily, I narrow my eyes and gauge his reaction when I ask, "Why would the force allow you to keep your equipment?"

"They didn't. I stole it."

"And they're not coming after you for it?"

"I'm not a threat to them. They think I've gone soft."

"Which gives you the advantage," I say.

"It gives us the advantage," he clarifies, letting me know he wants to work with us in the war against wolves. I mull that over for a minute longer and realize that under the circumstances I know I have no choice but to let him into my small circle. It might be the only way we can find the others.

When a vehicle slows on the highway, I stiffen and shoot a nervous glance at my team. "We're drawing attention."

"Okay," my father says as he steps back, "We need to get out of here."

With that we all retrace our steps back to the vehicle, but my father slows and waits for me to catch up to him. He has a strange, nervous energy about him, and it makes me antsy.

I glance up at him. "What?" I ask.

"We need to hunker down for the night."

"Where do you suggest we go?"

His mouth turns down in a frown, and he kicks at the gravel beneath our feet almost apologetically. "There is only one place we can go."

I look at him, but I'm not sure what he's suggesting.

He touches my arm to still me as everyone else climbs inside the SUV. "Pride," he begins his voice full of remorse and when I see the lines around his mouth tightening, I know in an instant where he's taking us. I stiffen and shake my head.

"I don't think—"

"We need sleep." His glance flickers to the inside of the vehicle and he knows he's hitting a sore spot with me when he adds, "They need somewhere to go and Sandy doesn't look well."

I angle my head to see the young girl and when I do, my stomach tightens. I know she's seen a lot, been through a lot, but I thought once I got her away from the master and gave her a taste of freedom, it would help her heal. Maybe this new world and all the threats in it are too much for her to handle in her condition.

"Sandy needs food and sleep," I announce, and while there are so many things I don't know about my father's motives, I do get the sense that he's trying to do right by me. I still have no idea what suddenly prompted him to change his ways, but I understand he is trying to right his wrongs and forge some sort of father daughter relationship between the two of us. What I don't know, of course, is why now.

His voice is uncertain, his eyes so sad and regretful when he asks, "So you're going to be okay going back to my place in the hills?" that it has me craving to claw back the years we lost, has me aching for my mother's comfort.

I miss her so much.

I miss her touch, her scent, the way she always made me feel safe even when I knew we weren't. As my chest fills with heartache, I swipe at my eyes and turn from my father, not wanting him to see any weakness in me as I think about the family I lost.

I know I made the hard decision to try to better understand him, to learn from the man whose blood runs through my veins, but as I think about stepping into the mansion where my father once imprisoned wolves, to come face to face with the things he's done to our kind, I'm suddenly not so sure that I'll ever be okay again.

8

A tremor moves through me as my father drives the vehicle along the winding driveway leading to his mansion. I briefly shut my eyes and when I open them again, I glance over my shoulder to catch one last glimpse of the world I'm leaving behind, and try to fight the strange sense that I'll never see it again.

An ominous feeling settles in the pit of my stomach as the heavy metal gate clangs shut behind us. The site is so hauntingly familiar that it brings back horrific memories of my dark days in captivity.

Beside me, Stone squeezes my hand tighter, and even though I keep my expression blank, vacant, he's still fully aware of the knot weaving itself tighter and tighter in my stomach.

"*It's going to be okay,*" he whispers inside my head, but from the tension in his body, I know his stress levels are every bit as high as mine.

Floodlights ignite the compound and bathe the huge expanse of lush, green lawn in artificial brightness. When I get my first real look at the impressive house where my father once kept wolves under his strict command I suddenly feel a little nauseous, a little overwhelmed.

As my mind shifts and sorts through this unexpected turn, mental images of all the cruelties that took place in this compound play out in my mind's eye. Working to push down my emotions in an effort to keep all my wits about me, I draw in a fortifying breath to calm myself. But then I think about the first time Logan saw my battle scarred body and I remember what he said. His master wasn't cruel like mine.

As that last thought settles me slightly, and gives me a modicum of hope that deep inside my father has redeeming qualities, I canvass the perimeter and wonder if the high voltage gate locking the world out—and us in—is powered with electricity. If we have to get out in a hurry, will we all be electrocuted?

With old habits dying hard, I mentally catalogue the area, and search for an escape route. While I believe my father is trying to change his ways, and isn't out to harm us, it still doesn't stop me from approaching this change of plans with caution.

He parks at the top of the twisting driveway and after he slams the SUV into park, we all pile out and wait for my father to make the next move. A bird takes to the sky as he circles the vehicle to meet us on the cobblestone walkway leading to the front door. I breathe deep and catch the sweet scent of berries on the breeze. The familiar aroma elicits a shiver from deep inside me.

Looking tired, weather-beaten, and emotionally battered, my father's shoulders slump slightly when he announces, "There are enough bedrooms upstairs for everyone. Take your pick. We can talk in the morning after everyone is rested."

With that my father steps ahead of us all, and we follow

him to the front entrance where he punches in a code to open the door. I listen to the beeps and commit the numbers to memory. I don't miss the concentration on Stone's face, an indication that he is doing the same. Pushing past our fears, we all step inside.

Even though I'm tired, my body craving sleep, and my knees so weak they simply want to collapse beneath me, I know I'll never be able to settle myself down. I step farther into the foyer, my boots sliding over the polished marble floor as I take in the opulence of his estate.

"Alexander, is that you?" a male voice booms from the near vicinity.

I stiffen as a big, burly man approaches from the east wing, his beefy hand hovering over his gun as he carefully assesses us, stopping to size up each and every intruder. I shift my stance, and when I feel the gun I now possess scraping along my spine, it gives me a measure of comfort.

Once his inspection is complete he steps up to my father, and I take a moment to think about the name Alexander. I haven't heard my father's first name in so long that I'd almost forgotten he has one, almost forgot what it means. Defender of men. Too bad he's never lived up to it.

"What's going on here?" the guard asks, his booming voice echoing off the high ceilings and walls.

My father holds one hand up to calm the man I can only assume is his guard. "Everything is fine. We're all going to get some sleep and we'll talk in the morning."

The guard backs down and nods. My father turns to us, and gestures toward the staircase. "Go get yourselves settled in."

All eyes turn on me, waiting for me to make the next move. Since I know we have no other option, I give a quick nod of consent and we all tromp up the stairs. My stomach is a bundle of nerves and I wait until everyone finds a bed before I slip into the last room at the end of the hall. I quickly close the door behind me, needing to be alone to get my thoughts together.

I simply stand there for a long time, waiting, listening, but for what I don't know. I flick the light on, and walk the room, committing every piece of furniture, every obstacle and escape route to memory.

The silence in the house is almost deafening as I run my fingers over the wood dresser, the antique rocking chair in the corner, and the nightstand. When I step up to the bed, feel the lace on the bedspread, and take in the soft pastel color on the wall, I realize the room has a woman's touch. Did my father mate with someone after losing my mother, or is this simply the work of a caring housekeeper?

That last thought has me thinking of Mica, and for the first time in a long time a smile touches my mouth. She was always so kind to me, and if it wasn't for her I might never have made it to the master's dungeon to get the key that helped free us all. My heart aches to know that after all these years she is finally going to be free of the master's control and reunited with her family.

I remove the gun from my waistband, tuck it under my mattress and fling myself onto the bed, taking care to keep my dirty boots off the pretty covering. As I think about Mario and the others who helped me win the battle against our cruel master, a myriad of emotions erupt inside me. I stare at the stark white ceiling overhead, but I don't take pleasure in the soft mattress beneath me. The last thing I want to do is get too comfortable in this place.

Feeling restless, I turn on my side, and that's when I hear voices coming from the ventilation system. I listen, but can't make out the words, but there is no mistaking the angry voice of Logan ringing hollowly through the pipes.

I climb from my bed and tiptoe across the floor to put my

ear near the plastic slats. When I angle my head, I find myself staring at an antique nightstand, and there is something sticking out of the back edge of the drawer, some sort of picture that, judging by the yellowing corner, looks like it's been jammed in there for years, missing and forgotten.

Curiosity piqued, I crawl across the floor, carefully pull the nightstand away from the wall, and give a tug on the drawer to loosen whatever it is lodged in the back.

I carefully grip the corner of the picture and jiggle it back and forth until I loosen it. When I finally manage to free it, it slips from my hands and falls to the floor. I suck in a sharp breath and stare at the image for a long time, almost afraid to touch it. But when I finally reach for it, there is nothing I can do to stop the big hiccupping sob clawing its way out of my throat. I tentatively run my finger over the captured image of a very young, very pretty woman, one with a sad yet serious look on her face. When I flip it over and see the name Abigail scrawled on the back, along with a date, my heart turns over in my chest.

How? Why?

I consider the photo of my mother longer and as I wonder about the day it was taken, a million questions race through my mind. Was the picture taken before or after the master captured her and tossed her into the basement to live a life of confinement? Had my father picked her to be a part of his world because he loved her, or did he fall in love with her after he'd picked her?

What did my mother really know about him?

Remembering my mother has my chest squeezing in heartache, and my eyes filling with water. When my vision blurs, I drop the photo and pull my hands back like they've been burned, then look at my closed door. Feeling suddenly confused, and in desperate need of fresh air, I tiptoe across the wood floor, inch open my door and listen for sound. With no one moving about, I creep from the room, retrace my steps down the stairs, and punch in the code to the front door.

I rush outside, run away from the monstrous mansion, and suck in a huge breath and hold it until my lungs hurt. When I begin to feel lightheaded, I finally exhale and draw in quick sipping breaths to fuel my blood. That's when I catch the fragrant aroma of flowers. I scent the air for danger, and when I find none, I circle the mansion.

When I reach the back of the estate, instead of finding an obstacle course housed inside an imprisoned courtyard, I find a lush flower garden, and when I sink to my knees I suddenly feel so very tired, physically and emotionally.

When a dark shiver pulses in my blood, all I want to do is forget. Forget about those I've loved and lost. Forget about my failed mission to find the others, to stop the PTF. Forget about how much I've hurt the two boys who care so deeply for me.

But since it's not in my nature to forget, I pull the sweet perfume into my lungs, and let the memories flood me until I feel like I'm drowning.

But then another smell hits me from behind, pulling my thoughts to the present. I listen to the quiet approach, fully aware of his presence before he speaks.

"*Hey,*" the voice inside my head says.

I look over my shoulder. "*What are you doing out here?*"

"*I could ask you the same.*"

I shrug. "*Couldn't sleep.*"

"*Want some company?*"

"*Okay,*" I say, knowing we need to talk about what happened tonight, but not knowing where to start.

Taking care not to crush any of the flowers, Stone hunkers down beside me and his warm familiar scent curls around me and hugs my body like a tight sweater. After a long moment he says, "I'm sorry, Pride."

I look at him and my heart turns over in my chest when I see the sadness in his eyes. "Sorry about what?"

"For not catching up with Nova," he replies soberly.

There is a new darkness in his eyes and I feel a quiver move through me. "What would you have done if you caught her?" I ask tentatively, a little worried about his answer.

"I would have killed her." His words are delivered with such cold calculation it twists my heart and has fear shooting through me.

"You can't do that, Stone. You can't go around killing people."

"She threatened you, Pride. And that gives me every right to kill her."

I fist my hands until my nails bite into my skin and feel almost frantic when I say, "No. She made a mistake and I don't want anyone else to die. Not because of me."

"Her mistake was falling for Logan," he says, his voice holding a degree of anger, but there is no hardness in his eyes when he touches my chin and tilts my face until we're eye to eye. "But I guess we all make mistakes, and we don't always make rational choices when we're in love." He gives a humorless smile and adds, "Now that's something Nova and I have in common."

"Nova wanted to kill me to be with Logan," I say and before he can stop me, I push my way into his mind, wondering if he'd go so far where Logan and I are concerned.

I take a moment to process his thoughts, then my eyes widen, unease seeping from my every pore. "Stone," I choke out. "You can't just—"

"The master should have let me and Logan finish that fight. One day we'll have to, you know."

My heart pounds and I shake my head so hard, my hair flares around my face. "No. That can't happen."

"We can't have two alphas in the pack, Pride."

I swallow, because I know he's right and I also know the tension between the two is escalating, and if something or someone doesn't give soon, one of them is going to die.

Since I can't bring myself to think about that anymore, can't consider how much Stone would like to remove Logan from the equation, I redirect the conversation.

"Tonight," I begin. "At the cabin. You have to stop reacting where I'm concerned. It's different out here. We need to work together. It's not about protecting one person at the cost of everyone else." I reach for a blade of grass and my hair falls into my eyes as I run it over my lips. "What you did tonight, throwing yourself at that officer, it could have...it could have been bad in so many ways, Stone." I pull my knees up to my chest and try to find the right words. I look every-where and anywhere, unable to meet his eyes, unable to deal with the sadness I see on his face. "I understand why you did it, but out here things are done differently. I'm going to help guide you, help you change—"

"Pride," he says, cutting me off. I turn to him and he brushes my hair from my face until my eyes are uncovered... until my raw feelings are exposed. His glance isn't apologetic when he says, "I don't want to change."

I open my mouth to voice an argument, but stop when he jumps to his feet. "This is who I am," he hurries out, and I see a flash of possessiveness on his face as he begins to pace. "All I want to do is protect you." He stops abruptly, adjusts his footing and grabs my hands to haul me to my feet. When my body collides with his, he stands over me. Silence ensues as he looks at me with dark eyes that reveal his every emotion.

He finally breaks the quiet by saying, "It's all I ever want-ed." He touches a strand of my hair, and I suck in air when his warm knuckles brush along my face. "Is that so wrong, Pride?"

As I weigh his words carefully, my anger melts and I swallow hard. Life's events have shaped him into who he is and how he reacts, and while I know his thoughts and actions aren't really wrong, I also know they're not quite right either. But how is any of that his fault?

He moves inside my head, the connection between us tremendous as he pulls me impossibly closer, his hands crushing my hair. "*Pride*," he whispers. "*All I want to do is take care of you.*"

A low moan that sounds more wolf than girl ripples in my throat. I struggle to keep myself together when I say, "*And that's the problem Stone.*"

"*Why?*" he asks. "*Why is that so wrong?*"

"*Because our world is changing and we're part of a bigger picture. We all have to take care of each other. You're wearing blinders when it comes to me and I'm afraid your tunnel vision is going to get you, or someone else, killed.*"

The dark shadows under his eyes deepen and he makes a deep animal sound full of need when he counters with, "*If I have to die, then I'd gladly die for you.*"

"*You don't have to die. I don't want you to die.*" I lower my eyes and emotions fracture my voice when I admit out loud, "I...I couldn't handle it if anything happened to you."

I listen to his sharp intake of air. "Nothing is going to happen to me."

"It will if you don't stop doing stupid things." I close my eyes against the flood of emotions and pound on his chest. Stone grabs my fist to stop me, and what he does next has a sob rising in my throat.

"Everything I do is to protect you." He holds my hand over his heart, and the intensity on his face is almost frightening when he says, "Because this belongs to you, Pride. It always has and always will."

"Stone—"

"Let's go."

"Go? What are you talking about?" I ask, confused by the abrupt change in conversation.

"Over there." He gestures with his chin toward the hills behind us and takes my other hand in his as he transfers his thoughts to mine. "*Me and you. Right now. Let's get out of here.*"

I give a fierce shake of my head, and inch back, wondering if anything I just said actually registered with him. Rooting my feet, I answer with, "You know I can't do that. I can't turn my back on these wolves."

His eyes cloud, and his look is wounded. "You know I'd never ask you to do that. I'm only asking you to run with me. Tonight. Let's free our wolves from their leashes." He steps back into my personal space and pulls me closer until my body is smashed against his. He tangles his hands through my hair and dips his chin, his eyes are full of possession as tenderness steals over him. "Let me prove to you that you belong with me. That we belong together."

I feel the tension rising in him and before I realize what he's doing, his lips close over mine. He kisses me with such savagery it occurs to me just how lost he is.

"Please, Pride," he whispers into my mouth, his voice playing down my spine as he draws me in to a place where emotions rule.

My heart leaps and my wolf wails, because I know what he's asking. What he wants our fated wolves to do. I open my mouth to speak, but have no idea what it is I want to say.

He runs his hands along my back and an unexpected curl of heat wraps around me. I wail, because I know what's causing my blood to burn, my skin to come alive. My wolf is programmed to seek her destined mate, but how can I possibly give Stone what he's asking for when I've already offered myself to another.

I feel him inside my head once again, attempting to probe. I block him and stumble to speak, but before I can get any words out, Stone's shoulders square and his entire body stiffens like he's preparing for a fight.

My mouth slams shut and when he looks past my shoulders, I turn to follow his gaze, fully expecting to see Logan. I spot movement in the shadows and when I catch a foul scent in the breeze, I instantly know who has invaded our privacy.

Footsteps fall mutely as my father comes closer, and I don't need the artificial floodlights scanning the area to see the dark torment on his face.

"We've been searching for you. You need to come inside," he says, and I stiffen, the worry I hear in his voice triggering a reaction from my wolf.

I brace myself. "What's going on?"

"It's Sandy. She needs your help."

"Sandy?"

I exchange a quick look with Stone then hurry past my father, ribbons of fear trickling through my blood. I know she insisted on accompanying us to Lewis Lake, but I never should have agreed.

"Where is she?" I call over my shoulder.

"She's in her room."

I take the steps two at a time and burst through the door to Sandy's room. The first thing I notice is the scent of blood. It's so strong, the coppery tang saturates the air and settles on the back of my tongue. I swallow hard and try not to gag as I take in the scene before me.

Perched on the bed, I see Logan talking to Sandy, his voice is low, soothing. Gem turns my way. Her face is full of anger and grief. Without speaking, she steps around me carrying an armload of blood soaked towels.

My stomach cramps, and my hand closes over my mouth to stifle a gasp.

"She's taken pills. She found them in my medicine cabinet," my father whispers in my ear as he and Stone step into the room behind me. "The bottle is empty. She must have taken at least twenty."

"What kind of pills?" I ask and shoot him a glance.

His lips are pinched tight, and the white lines circling his mouth are a clear indication that whatever she ingested could very well be the end of her.

"Acetaminophen," he finally says.

I try to keep the panic at bay as I think back to my lessons with Ms. Kara. She taught me all about the deadly side effects of acetaminophen. If a cat or dog ingests too much, it can become toxic. Except wolves aren't dogs and we have regenerative abilities. At least mature wolves do, which has my mind racing to Sandy's baby. They could never withstand such huge amounts of poison. Sandy knows that every bit as much as I do. As I consider that, it becomes achingly apparent that she knew what she was doing, that her action had been on purpose.

I fight down my rising hysteria and draw a breath to center myself, but there is nothing I can do to keep guilt from eating at me. I should have paid closer attention to her. I should have been more aware.

I step up to the bed and the cushy mattress sinks a little as I sit down next to her.

"Sandy," I say gently and brush her damp bangs from her forehead. I squeeze her other hand, a silent apology for all the things that are happening to her. For all the things that happened back at the compound.

For all the things I couldn't stop from happening.

Frustration and helplessness hit at the same time and it

takes all my effort to keep my voice level when I ask, "How are you feeling?"

With uncoordinated movements, she clutches the mattress and her fingers curl into the sheets beneath her. That's when I see how swollen her face is, how her actions are stiff, clumsy.

"Is it gone?" she asks, and I don't miss the note of desperation in her voice.

I brush tiny beads of moisture from her face, and as she stares at me, her eyes wild, delirious, I know the toxins have yet to push their way through her body. I turn to see Stone and think about the way he once helped me fight the poison in my body. By angering me.

Knowing that isn't the solution for her, I think back to my lesson. "She needs hydrogen peroxide." I have no idea if it will actually help nullify the effects, but I know anger is the last thing she needs to be feeling right now. Stone gives a nod then exchanges words with my father before he disappears into the hall.

"Is it gone?" she asks again around a thick tongue.

"Yes," I say, my glance going back to Logan's and I watch the muscles along his chin clench as his jawbone seesaws from side to side. "It's gone." After Logan gives me a pained frown, I ask, "Do you want to tell me what happened?"

"He's out there. I know it. I can feel him."

I don't have to ask to know who she's afraid of most. "He's not out there, Sandy," I say and continue to smooth her hair from her face. "We've been over this. The panthers took care of him."

"No. You're wrong," she rushes out, her body shaking, her head tossing back and forth almost frantically. "I can feel him."

Logan and I exchange a worried look, and I adjust my position on the mattress to lean closer. I capture her head between my palms to still her and try to get her to focus her thoughts.

"How can you feel him?" I ask, my stomach turning because I'm suddenly not sure I want to hear the answer.

"Because...because of our connection," she admits, and looks down almost sheepishly.

Hearing that one word has my world tilting on its axis, and I feel a desperate sort of anger inside me. My hands slip from her face, and while I'm afraid I already know the answer to my next question, I know I still have to ask it. I need to hear her say it.

I capture her shoulders and try to sound more in control than I feel. "What kind of connection, Sandy?"

She blinks up at me and her words are slow when she says. "It...it...was his."

My breath leaves my lungs in a whoosh, and my limbs feel numb as my blood drains to my feet. As I rationalize and digest her words, my wolf howls to break free and run. Beside me I can almost hear Logan's mind reeling, and in an attempt to connect with him mentally I search around for him in the dark. His head comes up with a start, and while we can't speak telepathically, I get the oddest sense that he can still feel me.

I mouth the words, "She needs to shift."

"The poison in her body won't allow it," he answers quietly. "She has to ride it out."

I take a moment to consider this turn of events, then quickly berate myself. I should have put it together. The master had broken her, and she wanted to please him. From the intimate, adoring way she was acting with the man who controlled us, I should have realized what he'd done to her.

When a big hiccupping sob cuts the quiet around us, I say, "Okay, Okay. Everything is going to be okay."

Acting purely on instinct, I gather her into my arms.

Mimicking the way my mother used to try to soothe me, we rock back and forth on the bed, and while I know so very little about comforting someone, I try to do right by her. She deserves that much from me.

"He's going to come for me," she says through a frightened sob as she clutches my arm. "And he's going to be angry." She inches back, and her nose is red and swollen, her lips horribly chewed. "But I couldn't let him have it, Pride. I couldn't."

"I understand."

She nods and sniffs, her dark eyes hopeful, searching for approval. "You do?"

"Of course I do and I won't let anyone hurt you. Not ever again."

"Okay," she manages to say, her lids drooping around her eyes as sleep pulls at her. As she comes in and out of consciousness, I can feel her frustration, helplessness, confusion. We stay like that for a long time, and just when I think she's fallen asleep her lids jump open.

"Pride," She says, her eyes rolling around her head like runaway marbles.

"Yeah?"

"I'm sorry. I didn't mean...I shouldn't have..." She blinks wet lashes over stricken eyes. "I did what I had to in order to survive. I didn't know you were going to come back to the compound to get me."

As I wonder what she's getting at, every nerve in my body stands on high alert, and the hairs running along my nape begin to tingle.

Before I can ask exactly what she's getting at, exactly what she *had* to do, she sags against me. I feel the fight go out of her body and fire burns my blood.

I touch her shoulders and gently ease her back onto her pillow, but when our eyes meet my heart begins to beat faster, and while I know I'm not going to like her answers, I'm suddenly desperate to hear them.

I let out a slow breath. "What I don't understand, Sandy, is why he would do this to you. He's human and he wanted to breed strong alphas into the pack. So why would he want to dilute it with a half breed offspring?"

"I'm, I'm not sure," she slurs, then she smiles likes she's remembering a distant past. "He promised me things. Nice things," she adds, but as I sit here and listen to her, there is a small intuitive part of me that says she's not being completely truthful.

She's not telling me everything.

As I consider our former master, a hard man driven by hate and greed, I know there is a purpose to his every action. He impregnated Sandy for a reason. I just don't know what that reason is.

After Stone comes back with the hydrogen peroxide, I take it from him, and pull Sandy to a sitting position. "Stay with me a little longer, Sandy. I need you to sip this."

I put the bottle to her mouth and she takes a few mouthfuls. Once I'm satisfied that she's ingested enough of the antidote I ease her back onto her pillow, and she exhales in an exhausted heap.

Gem touches my arm. "I think she needs to rest, Pride." With that she drapes a cool cloth over Sandy's forehead. "I'll stay with her."

I offer Gem a grateful smile, and force my feet to carry me out of the room. Once we all reach the hall, I look at Stone, the only boy who knows the master as well as I do.

I talk to him silently. *"There is more isn't there?"*

"Y*eah*," he agrees. *"There's something else she's not telling us."*

"*I know*."

I take a moment to think about what Sandy *did* tell us. The master promised her things. Nice things. My stomach cramps and the hairs on my nape tingle because the master never gives without taking.

So what did he want in exchange?

I mull that over a moment longer and realize Sandy was going to give him offspring, some sort of half breed pup. As I toss that around inside my head, a more frightening thought strikes.

What if it wasn't a half breed at all?

9

With that last thought bouncing around inside my head and filling me with a new sort of anxiety, I step away from the others to slip into the small bathroom near my bedroom. The lock clicks behind me as I listen to everyone file back into their respective rooms, leaving Sandy in Gem's care.

I move across the warm marble floor and grip the pedestal sink hard enough to turn my knuckles white. With my blood draining to my feet, I lean forward and draw deep breaths before lifting my eyes to stare at my reflection in the vanity mirror. My long hair falls forward in a tangled mess around my chalky face, and I don't miss the horror in my dark eyes or the inky smudges beneath them as I consider the root of Sandy's fears.

Is it possible that she turned the master? Created a new kind of monster and unleashed him into the world?

Even though I'm on edge, a yawn pulls at me, a reminder that I haven't had a decent night's sleep in ages. I blink to keep my eyes open and understand there is a real possibly that I might never sleep again—especially if Sandy created a dangerous new alpha.

Needing to sort matters through, I turn the cold water on and splash my pale face to help clear the fog from my tired brain.

If I'm right, if the master promised her nice things so she'd turn him, for reasons I've yet to understand, what suddenly prompted him to do it?

Why now, after all this time would he ask one of his broken wolves to change him?

From everything I've learned, wolves rarely turn humans, and when they do, it's through a careful selection process. The human candidate would only be turned if they could bring something new to the pack. But of course, I can't forget that none of those rules would apply in the master's house.

My mind takes me back to my last few days in his mansion. There were no indications that he'd been bitten, no signs, no scent variations, or behavioral changes that illustrated he was becoming wolf.

I take a minute to consider the time frame. If Sandy changed him in between moon cycles, when I was making my way back to the compound then it would have been too soon for him to display any changes. He wouldn't have any wolf strength or characteristics until he'd gone through his first full moon transformation.

That thought has me breathing a small sigh of relief. Because if he hadn't gone through a lunar cycle yet, it meant the feral panthers would have easily taken care of him. He never would have survived long enough to reach the next full moon—a mere day ago—when he would have fed and become a full-fledged wolf.

Despite what Sandy said, despite her *feeling* him out there somewhere, he has to be dead. He just has to be. Otherwise...

A shiver moves through me, because there can't be an

otherwise. An otherwise means he's still out there—in wolf form—and that possibility is too horrific for me to consider.

I turn the water off, dry my face and hands on the big fluffy cotton towel beside me and draw a breath before opening the bathroom door.

I face a dark hallway, but the thoughts of returning to my room where I found an old, lost photo of my mother makes me feel restless, anxious.

I take a step, and when my booted feet thump on the floor, I stop and cringe.

Wanting to move about the house silently, I kick off my boots, and place them inside my room. But when I do, I once again hear voices coming from the ventilation system.

I walk to the grate and hunker down to listen. This time I'm able to make out what Logan is saying. And I'm able to determine who he is talking to.

"She deserves to know," Logan says, and even though his voice sounds tinny coming through the pipes, I don't miss the anger in his tone.

"When she's ready," my father counters and I hear a wheeze in his throat, like he's having difficulty drawing in air.

"Ready? And how much time do you think you have?"

I hear a scuffle, and my stomach tightens with worry as I continue to listen, wondering what is going on. What are they keeping from me?

But then my worry turns to anger, because I'm so tired of all the secrets. I might expect it from my father, but after everything we've been through, the only thing I expect from the boy I mated with is complete and utter honesty.

"Not enough time," my father answers, sadly. "Never enough time," he says again, and I don't miss the melancholy in his tone.

I hear Logan exhale slowly, and can almost feel the fight drain out of him. "Then you'd better do right by her and help her find her way before it's too late. She's counting on you, and after the life you let her live, she deserves at least that much from you."

The venom I hear in Logan's tone pulls a gasp from me, and I realize I'm seeing another side of the boy I mated with, a side that has my heart swelling with everything I feel for him.

As I consider the boy who crawled into my hell to help save me, my anger melts. I trust him with all my heart and realize he isn't keeping the truth from me on purpose. He's keeping secrets because he has to. Because he's protecting me from something. Something that has everything to do with my father.

It also occurs to me that if he's keeping something from me, then maybe I'm not ready to face it.

That dark thought sends my emotions on a roller coaster ride and the desperate need to find Logan prompts me into action. I climb to my feet and retrace my steps back into the hall.

Moving with stealth, I pad silently down the long winding staircase in search of the two. With the others asleep, I walk around the mansion undetected, and examine my father's belongings as I search him out. I step into the kitchen and open and close the drawers and cupboards. I make note of all the things I can use as a weapon if need be, and commit the contents to memory. Then make my way down a long hallway to find a heavy door leading to the basement. I stare at it, and my wolf growls, hating the thoughts of what that area once held.

Could they be down there?

I run my hand along the door frame, and look at the key pad beside it. When I realize it's been disabled and try the door, only to find it open, my heart gives a little lurch.

The hinges creak as I slowly pull it open, and the scent of

fresh pine hits with a slap. As I breathe in the cleaning solution, and note the freshly waxed floors, I move down the long corridor and don't miss the cameras pivoting to watch me.

I open a door leading to the basement, and when the scent of wolf, barely masked by the cleanser, rises up to meet my nostrils, I work to get my own wolf under control. Deep inside she's howling, urging me to run the other way because she knows.

She knows this is where my father once caged wolves.

Once caged Logan.

"Pride, don't go down there."

I spin around and find Logan moving toward me. His eyes are dark, his expression pained.

"Logan," I say, my emotions in a tangled mess as he pulls me away from the door and into his warm embrace. "This is where he kept you caged," I rush out.

Even though he can't read my thoughts, he's still privy to my concerns, and what he says next gives credence to our connection. "He never hurt me, Pride." His voice falls off and he runs the soft pad of his thumb over the scar on my neck, and when his eyes travel back to my face, what I see in his eyes nearly becomes my undoing. "Not like your master did."

I look over his shoulder, half expecting to see my father coming down the hall.

"Where is he?" I ask.

"I don't know."

"I heard you two talking."

His look is confused for a moment then his muscles tighten when he asks, "What did you hear?"

"I heard you telling him to do right by me." I want to say more. I want to ask questions. But I don't. While it's not in my nature to back away from the truth, I bite my tongue because I trust Logan. Trust that he knows what he's doing.

He opens his mouth like he wants to say something, then

seems to think better of it and asks, "What are you doing down here?"

"I was looking for you and my father."

Worried eyes search mine. "You shouldn't be down here. There is nothing here for you to see."

"Why are you down here, Logan?"

"I went to your room looking for you. And when I couldn't find you, I had a feeling."

"Am I that transparent?"

"I know the way you think."

"Then you must know I'm sorry for all this."

"You have nothing to be sorry for. I do."

I look at him, confused. "I'm the one who dragged you into all this."

"Hey, come on," he says, panic easing from his expression. "You didn't drag me into this. A few months back I came here on my own free will, remember. Then when I heard about the fearless Pride, I came looking for you." He pauses for a long moment, and emotions thicken his voice when he says, "The truth is, Pride, you could be dead because of me. You tried to tell me about Nova, but I didn't listen." He rakes his hair from his forehead and his glance is apologetic. "I just thought..."

"This isn't your fault. You've been through a lot these last couple of days and she's a member of your pack. Betraying you is the last thing you expected from her, especially after everything that happened at your village."

"I still should have known."

"She fooled us all, Logan."

"She didn't fool you." His nostrils flare and I feel his muscles bunch beneath me when he adds, "Or Stone."

"We've been caged and tortured our whole lives, and that makes us react differently."

He looks away, like he's unable to meet my eyes. "Maybe

he's right. Maybe he does know how to take care of you better."

"Logan," I rush out. "You once told me we were equals, and that it's our job to take care of each other. I love how you trust me, respect my choices and have such faith in me. It gives me faith in myself, and makes me stronger."

He grips the back of my head. "Pride, if anything ever happened to you..."

"Nothing is going to happen to me," I say, and swallow down my apprehension.

He pulls me in tight. "You're right. Because I won't let it. I made a mistake and it won't happen again." He splays his hands over the small of my back. "I don't know...I couldn't..." he says then stops like he can't force the words out of his mouth.

"I know, Logan. I know," I say. And I do know, because I couldn't face a future without him in it, either.

He looks at me long and hard and worry creeps into his voice when he says, "You need sleep."

When I think about returning to that bedroom alone, my heart pounds harder in my chest, and my legs tighten, refusing to budge.

Logan's face softens and, astute wolf that he is, he slips his arm around my waist. "Come on."

"Where are we going?"

"Outside."

"Why?"

"Because I know what you need."

Instead of asking what he's getting at I allow him to lead me out the back door. We move away from the house and follow a path leading toward a beautiful in-ground pool, and for some reason the water reminds me of the ocean and the promise Logan once made to me.

When the cool evening air wraps around me, he hugs me to him, and my wolf takes pleasure in the warmth of his body.

In the near distance the water ripples on a breeze, and we stand there in silence for a long time, both of us lost in our thoughts, and I wonder what he's thinking about when he angles his head and smiles at me.

He finally breaks the quiet and says, "Remember when we were in the woods?"

"Yes."

"What do you remember most?"

I instantly think back to the night I gave myself to him in the cave. I look at him, and he has a crooked grin on his face.

"Besides that," he says and rolls his eyes playfully.

I think for a moment then say, "I remember the bear that nearly killed me. I remember meeting the other kids and eating around a fire." I stop to give a frightened shake before adding, "I remember the PTF officers that nearly found us, and I remember you teaching me all about survival." I also remember him teaching me how to laugh, and how to cry, but I keep those thoughts to myself.

"Well, I'm in your world now, Pride." He shrugs. "So to speak. So why don't you teach me something?"

I look at him and know what he's doing. Even though he's worried sick about his family, his destroyed village, he's trying to distract me, trying to lighten my mood.

"I don't have anything to teach you."

"Sure you do."

"No. I don't."

Refusing to let it go, he says, "When we were pups we used to play games with each other. What did you do when you were a pup?"

I think back to the days when we were in the nursery, before the master turned us into feral watchdogs. "Well, there was this one thing we used to do, but it's kind of lame."

"Teach me."

"When we were let outdoors to socialize we would all search for the biggest, thickest blade of grass." I stop to look around. When I find one, I pluck it from the ground and say, "Here, like this."

"What did you do with it?"

I smooth the blade out, and position it between my thumbs, and then I blow into it until a shrill noise echoes around us.

"That's a mad skill, Pride," he teases and when I catch his grin, it reminds me of Logan's boyish, playful side, a side I haven't seen in a long time. A side I miss terribly.

I hand him the blade. "It' not as easy as it looks, you know," I respond, feigning hurt.

When he doesn't take the blade, I say, "What, are you afraid you can't do it?"

"No. It's just that you were right."

"About what?"

"This is kind of lame." With that he laughs, and the sound is so blissful, so magical, I find myself laughing right along with him.

He gives me a crooked smile full of mischief and my heart turns over in my chest. Even though I've spent the better part of my life hardening myself, after two minutes with Logan I find myself forgetting about the real world for a moment.

A noise sounds in my throat and as I shelve my worries for the time being, I shake my head. "How is it you always know what I need?"

His smile softens, and the corner of his mouth turns up, but there isn't a trace of humor in his voice when he says with absolute conviction, "Because I'm your mate, Pride."

Everything in the way he says mate, with such total confidence, such belief in me, in us, has my blood racing a little faster, and my throat tightening with emotion. While we might not have been born to be destined mates, it still doesn't mean we don't share a special bond.

"Okay, since your game was so lame, let me show you what we did as pups."

My throat feels swollen, too tight to talk, so I simply nod.

"Here are the rules. Whoever can make the other person laugh first wins."

He turns away from me, and when he looks back, his eyelids are flipped inside out. The horrendous sight has my head jerking back with a start and instead of laughing I pull a disgusted face.

"That's just wrong, Logan."

He blinks and his lids go back to normal. He clucks his tongue but his voice is playful when he says, "You're a hard nut to crack, Pride. I used to always win with that one."

I turn from him, and use my index fingers to pull the corner of my eyes down and my thumbs to push my nose up. I spin back around and Logan shrieks, the sound so high pitched and girlish we both end up laughing.

He grins. "Looks like it's a draw."

"No, I'm pretty sure I won," I announce.

"Fine you win," he says and juts his chin outward, like a spoiled child.

"So what does the winner get?" I ask.

"It was usually a stick of gum, but you, Pride," he says, his voice dropping an octave as his blue eyes darken with need. "You can have anything you want."

As I think about what I want, I ask, "What do you want, Logan?"

"Oh, I think you already know that." With that he throws himself on the ground and reaches for me. "Come here," he says and pulls me down beside him. With our arms and legs in a tangled mess, we lie there and look up at the stars, and while I appreciate the fact that Logan isn't putting any demands on me, there is another side of me that craves his touch, his kisses.

"You know, when this is all over, I'm going to make sure you laugh every day."

My stomach knots because my old fears that this war on wolves will never be over, haunts my thoughts. As I think about all those I've lost in battle, I say, "There was a picture of my mother in my room."

"I saw it when I went looking for you, but I didn't know it was your mother." He leans into me, plants his elbows on the ground and props his head onto his palm. "Although I should have known. You look like her."

"Why do you think he has that picture?"

"Probably because he really did love her, Pride."

"Do you think he has any of me?" I ask before I can think better of it, and hate how needy I feel, hate how it actually matters—that I allow it to matter—or that it would mean so much to me if he did.

"I'm sure he does."

Logan places his hand on my stomach and spans his fingers. As his warmth transfers to me, I close my hand over his, my mind instantly rewinding to our time on the mountain, to when we held and protected each other while we slept under the stars.

"Logan."

"Yeah?"

"Sandy thinks the master is still alive."

I feel his body tense. "Do you?"

I angle my head to see him. "I'm not sure. I don't think so, but what if—" my voice falls off because I suddenly can't push the words past my lips, suddenly can't give the idea validity.

But I don't need to voice those worries for Logan to know

what I'm thinking. "Do you think she changed him?" I don't miss the silver in his eyes as he carefully searches the grounds.

"Even if she did, he wouldn't have gone through a lunar cycle before the panthers got to him."

"He's a dangerous man, Pride. And we can never underestimate him."

"I know," I say quietly and after a long moment I ask, "Why do you think he'd want to turn wolf? Why now, after all this time?"

"I don't know. Power maybe. Or maybe he thinks he can control us better if he's one of us."

I take a moment to think about it longer, before asking, "Do you think Sandy is going to be okay?"

"She needs time to heal. I think it will be better once we get her away from all this."

I crinkle my nose and ask, "Where will we go?"

"After we find Malcolm and the others, we'll head to the Jasper Mountains and try to find my pack."

I think about that for a moment longer, and as he holds me tight, smoothing my hair from my face, I realize how much I've missed our private talks. How right it feels to be held by him, even if he was never destined to be my mate.

"Once we're all together again, we'll have to rebuild our lives."

Thinking about rebuilding has me remembering what Stone said to me only a few short hours ago.

"There can only be one alpha in the pack."

I think about how Logan went after Stone tonight, to bring him back to safety, and I wonder if Stone would have gone after Logan. And if he had, would two wolves have emerged from the ominous forest tonight? Or only one?

10

Many hours later a flock of chirping birds pulls me from my slumber, and I blink my eyes open to once again find myself all wrapped up in Logan.

I stretch and pull the fragrant autumn air into my lungs, letting it fuel my mind, body and soul. As my stiff limbs protest after sleeping on the hard ground, I ease out from under the heavy arm draped across my stomach and pull myself up to a sitting position.

Warm autumn sunshine spills over us, and I tilt my face and drink it in for a moment before looking at the boy sprawled out on the ground beside me. When my glance moves over his handsome face, noting how sweet and innocent he looks when sleeping, I don't miss the quickening of my heart or the way my wolf stirs restlessly.

There is nothing I can do to keep the smile from my face or my heart from fluttering a little quicker when he blinks his blue eyes open. I see raw emotion in his gaze and think about the way he lightened my mood last night after so many things went wrong.

"This is getting to be quite the habit," I say and stretch my hands over my head.

"You do seem to drag me outdoors to sleep a lot." His grin is mischievous when he says, "You know, if this is some twisted way of yours to get me alone—"

I arch a challenging brow and cut him off. "You were the one who dragged me out here," I counter.

His grin is sheepish when he admits, "Okay, so I like waking up with you like this. I'd like to do it every day." Then he pats the ground and runs the dewy blades of grass over his palms. "Well, with the exception of only hard ground beneath us." He pulls a pained face and the sound of his joints groaning and popping makes me laugh.

Before I can tease him back and ask if he's gone soft on me, a commotion from inside the house draws my attention. Frowning in worry, I climb to my feet and Logan follows me up. We hurry to the mansion and when we slip inside the back door leading to the kitchen I find my new family seated around a table.

The delicious scents of bacon, eggs, toast and coffee hit at the same time and when my stomach grumbles it's a reminder that I haven't eaten since yesterday afternoon.

I spin on bare feet and find Gem hustling about the kitchen, and can't help but think how domestic she is, or that it would serve me well to take a few lessons from her. Someday I'll have to learn to cook to feed my own family. But thinking about family has me thinking how a pack can only have one alpha.

I give Stone a brief glance, but can't bring myself to meet his eyes after spending the night outside with Logan. But I don't need to see his face to sense how dangerous he is right now, don't need to meet his eyes to know he's watching me.

Feeling uncomfortable under his scrutinizing gaze, I turn

my attention to Sandy, who still appears skittish but at least has a bit of color on her face.

My gaze goes from Sandy to Blaze, and in the morning light I see how young and innocent she is. Her big brown eyes are wide and with her hands tucked under her legs she watches us all carefully, like she doesn't know what to make of the crew who came to her rescue.

But that has me thinking of her family. Where are they? How did she get separated from them?

The empty wooden chair beside her creaks as I lower myself into it and when her glance settles on me, I offer her a smile in an effort to put her at ease.

"Blaze," I say softly, to ease her into conversation before I get to the hard questions. "How are you feeling this morning?"

"I'm okay," she answers, then darts a nervous glance around. "I just want to go home."

Leading with her answer I ask, "Where is home, Blaze? Where is your pack?" Instead of answering, she gives me an odd look, like she has no idea what I'm talking about, so I refocus my questions. "How did you get captured?"

Her voice is slow, hesitant when she answers with, "The other night, during the full moon, these men shot me, and the next thing I knew I was waking up in that cage." Despite the warmth of the morning a shiver moves through her and she hugs herself.

"They shot you?" I ask, wondering how she's still alive. I instantly think about Nova. Could this little girl be another pawn, harnessed by the PTF to trap us?

She nods, and lifts her shirt to show the scar. When I examine the spot where her body rejected the bullet and healed itself my insides turn to ice because one thing becomes glaringly apparent.

"They didn't use silver," I say, more to myself than anyone.

Of course they didn't. Because they wanted her alive, so they could have a little fun with her.

"Where did they find you?"

"In an alley way."

Anger trickles through my veins, and my wolf howls. Why was this young girl out wandering the dangerous streets alone? Why would her pack allow her to do that? I calm my agitated wolf before asking the next question.

"What were you doing in an alley way?"

"It was the night of the full moon," she says, and gives me a look that suggests I'm seriously dense for asking such a question.

I think about it for a moment, my brain spinning, but when comprehension slowly trickles in, I try to keep the hysteria from my voice.

"You were hunting?"

When it occurs with dawning horror that this young girl was out hunting humans on shift night, like it was the most natural thing in the world for her to do, I push back in my chair, my vision going a little fuzzy around the edges.

As my stomach turns and my mind races with a million questions, I take deep breaths to calm myself and struggle to wrap my brain around what she's telling me. She doesn't fit the profile of a rogue killer, so why is she out hunting humans? Why isn't she being cared for by a pack?

At the head of the table my father clears his throat, and that's when Officer Sanford comes into the room and drops down in the chair across from me.

His eyes lock on mine. "What you fail to understand, Pride, is that not all wolves are good. For every well-meaning wolf out there, there is a rogue, which is why I assembled a team and wanted to change tactics in our approach."

As I digest his words, I look at Blaze. "Do you hunt every full moon?"

She nods, and there isn't a hint of remorse on her face. "Don't you?" she asks.

"Yes," I say quickly. "But not humans."

She angles her head like she doesn't understand.

"Where do you live? Where is your pack?"

"My mom and me have an apartment in the city."

"And she hunts on shift night, too?"

Blaze nods in response.

I lean toward her. "Blaze, do you go to school?"

She pulls a face, like such a suggestion is ludicrous. "My mom teaches me everything I need to know."

"And she taught you that killing humans is acceptable."

She nods again, then as if to justify it she says, "But only on shift night."

"Did she teach you that wolf communities exist, and these wolves work together and take to the woods on hunt night to avoid killing innocent humans?"

She shakes her head, and it's clear she has no idea what I'm talking about.

"Do you think killing humans is wrong?"

"It's what we do," she says matter-of-factly.

With my heart racing and my breath leaving my lungs in a whoosh, I look at Officer Sanford. "She doesn't know," I say. "She doesn't know it's wrong."

"And that's half our problem, Pride. While some rogues kill because they enjoy it, there are others out there who are doing what they do because it's all they know."

"We need to help them," I rush out. "We need to get them off the streets and integrated into packs that will teach them and take care of them before the PTF get to them first."

Officer Sanford scrubs his chin. "And how do we determine which wolves are good, and which aren't? Our orders are to shoot and to kill. There are no gray areas, Pride. Not in this line of work."

As I think about that, I think about my purpose for this mission. I set out to find Malcolm and the others and in pursuit of freedom I wanted to confront the PTF. I wanted to change the fate of our future.

But how can I ask the PTF to stop hunting wolves, when clearly some wolves need to be hunted? Don't humans deserve to be protected from those that have gone rogue? Or those that have no idea that their actions are wrong?

As I toss that around in my mind, and my brain works to come to terms with this new knowledge, I begin to wonder if I'm approaching this mission all wrong. Maybe what I should be trying to do is educate the force and teach them about wolf behavior, to help them determine which wolves are rogue and which ones needs saving.

I look at Officer Sanford. If the force refused to listen to a member of their own team, how then can I get them to listen to me? What must I do?

And the truth of the matter is, listening to me isn't enough. For me to *know* the right wolves are being hunted, I'd have to be out hunting the streets myself, following the scent of those committing atrocities against humans. While my run in with Nova wasn't a pleasant one, at least something good has come from it. I'm better able to identify the raw odor of deception.

I scan the room and that's when my glance lands on my father and I know in an instant this is what he's been trying to tell me. For humans to be safe, the PTF *are* needed. While some wolves just want to live normal lives, there are others out there that don't. Although I'm suddenly questioning what normal is, these days.

Another thing that occurs to me is that Officer Sanford is trying to make things right, but this mission is too big for him, the dangers too high for one man going it alone. That's when I understand more than ever that I have to try to convince the PTF to change their hunting strategies, to understand we're not all the same.

I take a moment to sort things through and knowing I can only deal with one mission at a time I turn my focus to locating Malcolm and the others. Right now finding them is top priority and once they're safe then I'll turn my attention to the PTF and the matters of the rogue wolves.

"If the panthers have your pack," Officer Sanford begins, as if sensing the shift in my thoughts, "and the PTF find them before we do, then they're all as good as dead. Information came through my radio the other day, and from what I heard, I know they're getting closer to finding the hideout."

Panic bursts inside me. "We need to find them first."

The chair slides across the floor as Officer Sanford stands. "I need to make my way back to my place to get my radio equipment."

When Gem puts a plate of food in front of me my stomach growls, but I'm suddenly in no mood to eat.

"I had a run in with these panthers," Gem says as she holds her hands over her stomach. "And if they do have Malcolm and the others, I think they might have killed them already."

"Not necessarily," my father pipes in. "From what we know, the dangerous drug cartel moving in from the south are the ones controlling the panthers, using them against us so they can take over our territory. My guess is they want to add the wolves to their arsenal. Why kill them when they can harness them?"

Stone grunts, his disgust apparent in his tone. "Spoken like a man who knows what he's talking about."

As Officer Sanford exchanges a look with my father, my father hands him the keys to the SUV then turns to Stone.

He doesn't comment on the remark. Instead he tosses him a cell phone and says, "You should go with him."

My head jerks back with a start, surprised by my father's suggestion. Why would he choose Stone to go on this mission, the wolf who nearly killed the one man on our side, the same man my father is now pairing him up with. As I watch on, I can't help but think this union is a mistake, can't help but worry what will happen when the two are alone in close confines.

Stone and Officer Sanford glare at one another, then after a long moment Officer Sanford gives my father a hard look and says through clenched teeth, "I've got this under control."

"And now I do too," my father adds, motioning for Stone to keep a close eye on the former PTF officer and to keep in contact at all times.

Stone climbs to his feet and his eyes move over mine before he turns. I stare at his back until he disappears from my line of sight. Once he's gone, I nibble on my bacon, only because I know I'm going to need my strength. Then I thank Gem for the food before I hurry to my room, needing time to think about Blaze, Malcolm, the war on wolves I might have no chance of winning, and this wide spread problem I had no idea existed until now.

Sure I knew rogues roamed the streets and occasionally turned to crime, but because I've been imprisoned my whole life, I had no real idea how desperate things have become. Had no idea there were so many wolves living amongst the population completely oblivious to the immorality of their crimes.

When I make it to my bedroom I begin to pace, anxious for Stone and Officer Sanford to return so we can get to the others before the PTF find and kill them all.

I see the picture of my mother, which is now on my nightstand. A shiver rushes through my blood as I pick it up and hold it against my chest.

"Pride."

My head jerks up to find my father leaning against my doorjamb.

"What?"

"Can I come in?"

I shrug and clearly that's good enough for him because a moment later he's grabbing the rocking chair from the corner, and pulling it toward me.

When he sits I look at him, and before I can help myself I blurt out, "Did you really love her?"

There is no hesitation in his voice, no indication that I shouldn't believe him when he says, "I really did."

"Did she know what you were? What you did?"

"No, none of the imprisoned wolves knew. I kept my real purpose a secret so I could socialize and integrate with the wolves and keep them under control."

I blow a long slow breath, and think about how it would have destroyed my mother to know the truth. "I'm glad she didn't know."

His face is sorrowful, regretful. "I suspect someday she will."

I crinkle my nose. "How?"

He looks heavenward. "When we meet again."

I nod in understanding, but suspect that won't be for a long time. Wolves live many, many generations, which has me wondering how long my father has been walking this earth. Before I can ask, he smiles and what he says next has my words lodging in my throat.

"The happiest day of my life was when you were born, Pride. I knew from the minute I set eyes on you that you were going to be something special."

When a bevy of emotions ambush me, I gulp air and press the picture of my mother tighter against my chest.

"I wish it could have been different. Maybe if I had your force and determination, I could have tried to take a stand against all this, against the man who controlled you every bit as much as he controlled me."

We go silent for a moment and I think about how much we all lost. Then what my father says next has me jumping to my feet.

"Someday when you have your own pups, you might better understand why I left. Maybe then you can find it in your heart to forgive me."

"I'm not having pups," I blurt out in a knee jerk reaction and walk to my window to stare out at the wide expanse of manicured lawn below. A movement in the distance catches my attention, and I narrow my eyes to discern the figure.

"Why not?"

With my chaotic thoughts pulling me in so many directions, I'm unable to give the shadow any more consideration. I spin to face him. "Because..." As I work to formulate a response, I think about the reason I swore I'd never bring pups into this world. Because never in a million years would I let my cruel master hurt anyone I cared about. But I'm no longer imprisoned, I remind myself, and that changes everything.

My mind instantly rewinds to my time in the woods with Logan, when he once asked me if it was with the right guy, if I would have a family.

When I think about the right guy I think about the two alphas who care so deeply for me and my stomach clenches.

"You're a fertile female, Pride, and if our species is going to thrive and survive, you'll soon have to choose a mate and carry on with traditions."

A noise outside my window pulls my attention and I'm

thankful for the distraction. I turn from my father and watch for movement, but that doesn't stop him from carrying on with his lecture.

His voice takes on a serious edge when he says, "When one wolf dies, another has to be reborn."

As I think about all the death I've witnessed in my short life, air leaves my lungs.

"You'll soon have to take your place at the head of the family."

I fight to steady the pulse thrumming in my throat, because I suddenly have the weird sense that my father is preparing me for something.

"And you can only find your place when you find your way and embrace the alpha you were meant to be with."

I twist back around and stare at him. "And who do you think that is?" I question, my voice lacking any kind of tolerance for this conversation.

"Your true mate will bring out the best in you. The one you need might not be the one you want." I glare back, hating all his cryptic answers.

Anger, frustration, and confusion hit at the same time and I'm unable to keep the emotions from my voice when I ask, "What is that supposed to mean?" I drop back down on my mattress and struggle to get myself under control but realize that as I work to become more human in this outside world, hiding my emotions is so much harder to do, now that I feel them so strongly.

"You'll know soon enough."

"What I know is that I was born with a bond to Stone, yet I mated with another," I shoot back.

"Sometimes bonds are tested, Pride. Broken even." He leans toward me as if to emphasize the importance of his next words, and that's when I'm hit with that same foul odor again. "And it's only then that new, deeper connections can be made."

While I think about what he's saying I hear a noise in the hall and when I glance up and see Logan standing outside my door I wonder how much he heard. But when I see the worried look on his face it has my hackles rising.

"What is it?" I say.

"You'd better come outside," he says, an edge of danger in his voice.

A look comes over my father's face, and I get the sense that he's fully aware of what is out there. My wolf bristles, because deep down, she knows too. We both rise but before we follow Logan down the stairs, my father grips my elbow and I turn to him.

"I know I have no right to ask anything of you, but I want you to promise me one thing."

My body tightens, because I'm not sure I can promise him anything. "What?" I ask.

"Someday when you do have pups, I want you to tell them about me. Tell them their grand-papa would have loved them."

Even though I'm not sure I can do that, the sadness on his face becomes my undoing and I give a quick nod. With that I tug my elbow free and hurry down the stairs after Logan.

I follow him out the back until we're surrounded by fragrant foliage and when he steps toward the gate, I move in beside him. He nods toward the mountains and I scan the perimeter and look for encroaching shadows.

"Breathe Pride," he says.

When I do, I'm immediately assaulted with the rancid scent of cat. My hackles spike and I growl low in response.

My father mumbles something under his breath and pulls his cell phone from his pocket. He slides his finger across the screen and as he speaks, I scan the grounds for immediate danger.

Sensing the panthers are organizing an invasion I drop low in preparation. That's when I realize Stone and Officer Sanford are still out there, and unlike last time when my master's mansion was surrounded by feral cats, and Malcolm and the others went missing, I'm no longer caged. This time I can let my wolf off her leash.

Determined to end this and find the others, I feel my nails lengthening, my wolf eager to give chase. My howl punctures the air and I grip the hem of my shirt, but a hand on my arm stops me.

"We're outnumbered," my father says. "Besides, they pose no threat to us right now. The fence is armed, and I have guards on duty." He nods toward the house and when I follow his gaze, I see his men on the rooftop. "Nothing or no one is getting in here today."

"And by no one, does that include Stone and Officer Sanford?"

When his hands clench and he looks at a distant spot on the mountain, I once again breathe deep. But when a very familiar aroma fills my lungs, the hairs on my nape prickle and I nearly gasp for my next breath.

I pull the crisp clean air in again, but the scent is gone, disappearing as quickly as it appeared. My senses go on high alert, and despite knowing my former master was killed at the hands of panthers, I can't shake the uneasy feeling that I just caught his scent.

That he just might still be out there.

11

Cold floods me and fear has my hackles spiking. Logan's hand captures mine in a strong, reassuring grip, and when I feel the incredible pull between us, my body absorbs the warm heat of his palm. As his supportive touch seeps under my skin, I angle my head to see him.

"What is it?" he asks, his blue eyes darkening in genuine concern.

I crinkle my nose and speak low. "I just...I think I caught his scent."

Logan inhales and pulls the morning air into his lungs. I watch his face as he deciphers all the smells and know I don't need to explain who I'm talking about for him to understand.

He exhales slowly and frowns. "I can't catch it."

"I can't anymore either," I answer and don't discount the possibility that the scent came from one of the cats who killed the man still haunting my nightmares.

"We need to get prepared," my father says, and with that Logan and I both turn our attention to my father and follow him inside.

Logan lets my hand go as we step into the mansion, and when we enter through the kitchen I see the others still seated around the table. Looking at their faces I realize the tension inside the house is as elevated as it is on the outside.

I think about the young wolves who are in need of protection and still can't shake the uneasy feeling curling around me, one that has me fearing something very bad is about to go down.

My mind races to strategize our next move. While I try to figure out the best course of action to keep the young ones safe, I look pointedly at Blaze.

I mull over my concerns and know there is one thing I'm certain of. Both Blaze and Sandy have been through enough and I don't want them with us on this dangerous hunt. But leaving them here, with panthers prowling outside—and possibly my former master—seems like an equally bad idea.

We inch away from the others and I know my father senses my distress when he says, "We'll need Gem with us since her connection with one of the panthers might prove beneficial, but Sandy and Blaze should stay behind."

"What if—"

"They're safer here. My men are on duty and there isn't a panther getting through that gate."

But what about a wolf?

Worry spikes my blood pressure and I look at Logan, my eyes searching his.

He nods and once again takes my hand in his. "I agree, Pride."

I toss that idea around in my mind for a minute before I concede half-heartedly. "Okay."

My father gives a curt nod. "Now that we all agree," he begins, "Let's get ready. It's time to go hunting."

Something in the way he says hunting sends a dark shiver down my spine, because while I know we have to search for the others, I also know we're up against two very dangerous, very different enemies. And one wrong move could mean the difference between life and death for any one of us.

A lump lodges in my throat as I consider that possibility but since I know now is not the time for emotions I strive to find my voice so I can question my father.

"What about Stone and Officer Sanford? How are they going to get back inside?"

"They're not," he answers.

While I'm not sure what he's getting at, I don't like the implication that we're going to leave them out there to their own fate. I root my feet. "We can't go without them."

"Wouldn't think of it," he says. "We need Sanford's intel." With that he pulls his phone from his pocket, and that's when I realize he had the foresight to toss one to Stone earlier. "We're going to take the underground tunnels to get out of here and have them meet us at my safe house."

Catching me off guard he steps up to me and stares at me long and hard. His eyes are dark and full of an emotion I can't quite identify when he pulls a strand of grass from my mussed hair. His fingers brush my cheek and his brows collide.

"You're so cold."

As I think about the chill that won't leave me, Logan slides me a look and steps closer to offer his heat.

My father tilts my chin to examine my features. His glance roams over me like he's committing my face to memory. Like it could very well be the last time he sees it. He attempts a smile, but it doesn't reach his eyes and that's when I notice how desperately tired he looks.

"It's going to take some time for Stone and Sanford to return with their equipment, so in the meantime why don't you get yourself cleaned up, rest a bit, then get yourself prepared."

After I nod, my father says, "There are a few last

minute things I need to take care of," and with that he punches a number into his phone and steps into the other room.

I ease my hand out of Logan's, and while I think a hot, sudsy shower is a great idea, I'm not sure I can bring myself to indulge in such a luxury when the others are out there in danger.

I look at Sandy, Blaze and Gem who are all perched on their chairs and watching us with worry. "I need to explain the situation to them," I say quietly to Logan.

"I will. You go shower." He tugs his grass stained t-shirt from his body and pulls a disgusted face. "I'm going to climb in once you're done."

I open my mouth and Logan presses his finger to my lips to seal my protest. "Just go, Pride."

Less than ten minutes later, I climb into the shower and let the needle-like spray wash over my body. Even though I twisted the nozzle to hot, and blistering steam has taken over the room, it still does little to thaw the chill that has taken up residency in my body, freezing me to my very core.

When I grab the soap and wash my body, I can't help but think about Logan and our time in the park, specifically when we washed the dirt from our skin in the hot springs. My mind revisits that moment, and I remember the way Logan kissed my scars, the way he showed me I was beautiful, inside and out. I think about how lost and broken I was, and how he put me back together.

As emotions crowd me, my throat tightens, and I hug myself, but there is nothing I can do to keep the strangled cry from rising in my throat. Knowing I need to get my mind on the mission and off my feelings before they get the better of me, I quickly wash my hair, turn off the water, and grab a big fluffy towel to wrap myself.

After knotting it under my arm, I slide open the shower

door, and when I see a familiar shadow stalking toward me in the steam filled room, I gasp out loud.

"Pride," Logan says, his soft whisper so full of emotion and raw need that all the air leaves my lungs in a whoosh. We stand like that for a long moment, both staring at each other, then something else takes hold of us. Something neither of us has any control over.

I'm not sure who moved first, but the next thing I know I'm in his protective arms and we're gripping each other, clinging so tight that my lungs feel like they're crushing beneath the weight. My heart is pounding so hard, the blood racing through my veins so fast, I'm sure every wolf in the house can hear the frenzied rush.

Logan tangles his hands through my wet hair and his hold is fiercely possessive as his lips hover close to mine. With my breath coming quicker, undisguised need moves over his face. He looks deep into my eyes, and I can tell from the way he's searching my face that he fears these could very well be our last moments together.

"Pride," he says again as his eyes fix on mine, and there is something so primal and raw in his voice that it shreds my defenses and has my wolf howling with primitive need.

"Logan," I respond and when his gaze zeroes in on my mouth, I run my tongue over my lips, starved for his kisses.

His breath scorches my skin and when the scent of him fills my nostrils, everything I feel for this boy bombards me with the force of a thousand silver bullets. My body begins shaking, and as I become lost in the alpha holding me close, I try to take a breath but find air harder and harder to come by. Driven by pure instinct, I go up on my tiptoes, answering the unasked question dancing on his parted lips.

His chest heaves and when his soft mouth closes over mine a tortured moan lodges in my throat. At first his kiss is warm, soft, exploring, but when I wrap my arms around him and hold him tight—like it might be the last time I'll ever get the chance—he deepens the kiss and pulls me impossibly closer.

His body presses against mine and I can feel the tension in his muscles as his lips move over my mouth with such urgency, such incredible, mind numbing need. I respond in kind, and savor this stolen moment between us because some part of me warns that I might need this memory to draw on later.

Hunger prowls though me, but it's a different kind of hunger, one that has nothing to do with food and everything to do with this boy. Losing all composure, I kiss him harder, and can feel his muscles bunch beneath my fingers.

Even though my thoughts are whirling out of control, I'm aware that his familiar touch and ravenous kisses are the only things capable of combating the ice inside me. This boy, and this boy alone, is the only one with the power to warm me.

...the one you need might not be the one you want...

As my father's warning words ping around inside my head, I lock them away to consider later and instead indulge in this moment, this kind yet powerful alpha. I let his warmth streak through me and when I open myself up to him, a low growl sounds deep in his throat.

We exchange kisses for a long time, and I can feel the erratic rise and fall of his chest before he breaks the intimate connection and inches back. He grips my shoulders and I watch his throat work when he swallows. His voice lacks the calm steadiness I'm accustomed to and I can taste his tension like it's my own when he says, "Don't take any chances out there today, okay."

"You either," I respond between labored breaths, and as I stare at him, and take in the silver shards darkening his eyes, I know he's feeling the same thing I am. That something bad is about to go down. My fingers curl in his shirt in a desperate attempt to keep him close. Keep him safe.

I hear a strain in his tone and a new kind of worry in his eyes when he warns, "Promise me something."

My body tightens and while I would promise this boy just about anything, I suspect he's about to ask for the one thing I can't possibly give him.

"What?" I ask.

"Don't put yourself in any danger because of me."

I give a fierce shake my head, and my stomach clenches. "You know you can't ask me to do that."

His nostrils flare, and there is an element of desperation in his voice when he says, "I am asking."

"Logan—"

"If anything ever happened to you because of me, I just couldn't..."

"Then can I ask the same of you?"

"No."

Apprehension curls through me and I pound on his chest. "How can you ask it of me when I can't ask it of you?"

He grabs my palms. "Because you can't."

"That's not an answer," I cry out, the tension between us mounting as steam swirls around our bodies and raises both the temperature and anxiety in the room.

"All right, then how about this," he says pitching his voice low as he takes on a new approach. "How about because I love you with everything I have inside of me, and I don't want anything to happen to you. You're my mate, Pride and I will die before I let any harm come to you."

When his words take the wind out of me, we both go silent and the potent look in his eyes when they latch on mine touches something deep inside me, something that I know there is no coming back from.

"Okay," I finally say, my voice a breathless whisper as the fight drains out of me. "Okay, Logan."

"Pride—" he warns, his eyes glinting knowingly.

"Okay," I say again, and give that one word a little more weight as I force it past my lips.

Shrewd eyes search my face. "Okay," he says, and then exhales slowly. He drops his arms and with a jerk of his head he gestures behind him. "You have clean clothes on your bed. Go get dressed and I'll come find you when I'm done."

I nod, simply because I can't seem to find my voice, and slip out of the bathroom while Logan takes his turn in the shower. I hurry to my room, pull on the mish mashed clothes rounded up for me, and take a moment to compose myself.

When I turn and catch my reflection in the mirror, I take a long time to look at myself, a long time to think about the cryptic things my father has said to me over the past few days. As I think about family, bonds, destined mates, the delicate fate of our species, and the importance of preserving our kind, I walk around my room.

I look out my window and scan for danger. When my glance comes up empty, I plant myself on my soft mattress and my stomach tenses when my thoughts turn to Stone.

Worry for his safety in a world where he's so incredibly lost, reminds me that he's in desperate need of my guidance, even though he says he doesn't want it, and isn't about to change. It also reminds me of the raw, unchecked emotion in his voice when he said he could never let me walk out of his life again. But the truth is, I need him every bit as much as he needs me.

When I left the compound, it was with the intention of finding myself and learning about my past before I could commit to a future. Even though I've only been with my father a short time, being here, in this house and finding that picture of my mother helped me understand where I've come from. I might have the blood of a rogue running through my veins but at least I now know I've come from love.

And I embrace that truth, and recognize that I was born out of something beautiful, I wrap my arms around myself and smile. It's that one little thing and what it means to me that wraps around my soul like a healing balm and helps me finally recognize where I belong in this chaotic, dangerous world.

I draw in air and when I glance up to find Logan standing in my doorway, his blue eyes studying me carefully, I feel a new calmness come over me because after everything we've all been through, and with everything we're all about to face, I suddenly know my place and the path I am supposed to walk in this foreign world. But more importantly, I know who I'm supposed to walk it with.

His smile is tentative, unsure, and from his look alone I know he can feel the shift inside me. When his fresh clean scent swirls around me, I climb to my feet.

"It's time," I say, but before I meet him at the door, I grab the gun stashed under my mattress.

Close to an hour later, after making sure Blaze and Sandy are both secure inside the mansion, we make our way to the mountain top. We negotiate the dank underground tunnels leading from the estate, and soon enough I find myself standing with my father, Logan and Gem outside the safe house at the peak of the mountain.

I watch the slow approach of my father's SUV and see Stone watching me through the windshield.

Always watching me.

When I meet his glance and see a bevy of emotions pass over his eyes, I know he can feel the shift in me every bit as much as the alpha hovering close.

12

The mood in the vehicle is somber as we listen to the hard voices coming through Officer Sanford's radio. When the PTF relay coordinates and mention they'll be sending out scouts before a full blown attack, my dry throat cracks.

Officer Sanford flicks off the radio and stares straight ahead. "The panthers have taken over one of the mansions they've invaded. We need to move."

My father puts the SUV into gear and pulls onto the Interstate. Silence ensues as we drive, each and every one of us lost in our own thoughts. I stare blankly out the window, and lean my head against the backrest, but when the chemical scent emanating off the treated leather seat fills my nostrils it reminds me I'm sitting on dead animal flesh. My entire body stiffens.

Thinking of dead animals has me worrying about the feral panthers we're about to encounter and the final fight that will surely ensue between cat and dog.

As I mull that over, I continue to watch the scenery speed by and close to an hour later, my father pulls off the highway.

He takes a long winding stretch of secondary road for a good thirty minutes before turning onto another path that will lead us to the lair.

Before we reach the sprawling estate, we pull the vehicle off the road. Since we'll have to complete the last of the journey on foot, and try to approach undetected, we camouflage the vehicle in the trees, and wait for complete darkness before stepping onto the shoulder of the road.

We trek forward and when we round a corner and see the sprawling mansion at the crest of a winding hill, Gem's eyes flicker beneath the rising moonlight. I watch her breathe deep to pull all the scents into her lungs.

"They're here," she announces, and all eyes turn on her. Her eyes meet Logan's and they exchange a knowing look before she exhales a breath of relief and says, "And they're alive."

I don't need to ask to know she's talking about Malcolm and the rest of her pack. I almost breathe a sigh of relief right along with her, but resist the urge. While I now know they're still alive, I also know it would be premature of me to believe they're going to walk away from this unscathed. After all, there's still a chance the PTF will get to them first.

Officer Sanford tucks his radio into his vest, and when I see his holstered gun, it reminds me of the one tucked in my waistband. While it might not kill a panther, I know it will slow one down.

This time Logan takes the lead, and picks up a pebble to test the metal gate surrounding the mansion. When no sparks light up the night sky, we walk the perimeter until we find the best spot to climb over. Once we're all inside, we make our way forward, all the while looking for signs of danger.

As I scent the air, I can't help but think how this feels so eerily familiar to me. Nor can I do anything about the bad feeling tainting the blood in my veins. Logan stops abruptly, and when my feet come to a resounding halt behind him and I catch the tang of his tension, I put a reassuring hand on his warm back.

When he turns to look at me the rancid tang of panther saturates the air and I can feel his wolf growling and clawing to break free, but we all know it's too soon to untie the tethers and release our primal sides.

Keeping downwind we move with stealth and as we stalk forward, I wonder if the panthers are in the mansion alone, or if they're with their handlers. It also makes me wonder what the handlers use to control them. For us wolves it was microchips, collars, abuse and intimidation.

With the mansion in full view, I look around at all the manicured shrubs and towering trees strategically placed in the back courtyard. My glance comes up empty, and while I know there isn't a single PTF officer in sight, it doesn't mean scouts aren't on their way.

"They're inside," Gem whispers.

I lower my voice to match hers. "Can you reach them? To find out what we're up against?"

"I'll try but I have to shift."

We all stand back while Gem calls on her wolf. A moment later her long nails rake the ground and a tormented whine sounds in her throat as she paces the exterior and tries to make a mental connection with her pack.

When she comes back to us, she shifts back to human and pulls her clothes on. "I can't reach them," she whispers, real fear on her face. "They're not in wolf form."

"Then we have no choice but to go in blind." I look at my father. "You and Officer Sanford stand guard out here and signal if you see anything." When they nod, I turn to the others and say, "As soon as we get in, Logan and I will go in search of them. Stone, you and Gem will have to cover for us."

Stone's nostrils flare. "I don't think we should separate."

"Stone," I begin, "I can take care of myself." I prepare to say more, to tell him he needs to trust in my strength instead of trying to be it, but then shut off my thoughts, knowing any argument on my part is futile. It doesn't matter what I say because I know Stone will risk his life—and the lives of the others if need be—in order to protect me. While I don't want that to happen, can't let that happen, I know there is nothing I can do to change the alpha wolf so set in his ways.

I work to address his worries. "It makes more sense for us to separate." When he gives me a quizzical look, I pause for a moment and try to deliver my next words as delicately as I can. "We'll need to communicate from separate rooms, and since we're the only ones who can do that in human form..." I let my voice fall off because from the hurt look on Logan's face I know I've said enough.

After a good show of agitation Stone says, "Fine, just keep yourself open to me," and with that he turns to Gem. We all walk the deathly quiet path leading to the back door and my father jimmies the lock and slides it open.

Once we're inside the pitch black mansion, I step over broken glass and notice how ransacked the place is. I take another quiet step and the fetid odor of cat clogs my throat. But this time I don't dare breathe through my mouth and miss their stealthy approach.

Gem inhales, then points to a door leading to the basement and that's when it occurs to me Malcolm and his pack are being held in the same kind of underground prison I once was.

When I see the broken keypad, I communicate with my eyes and Logan and I both step toward it.

With Logan's body close, we enter a dark tunnel leading to the underground chambers and when it feels like the walls are closing in on me, a very sick feeling mushrooms inside me.

I feel Stone probing my thoughts. *"Listen, Pride."*

With my senses finely tuned I hear the soft purr of cat coming from the ventilation system, and even though it should give me a measure of comfort to know the felines are asleep, it doesn't. Instead my skin begins to prickle and every wolf instinct I have warns of danger. And this time I'm going to listen.

Thanks to my encounter with Nova, I know better than to ignore my primal side. The last time I disregarded my natural intuition I walked straight into a trap and nearly ended up dead.

I swallow hard and reach out to Stone who is watching our backs from the other room. *"Something's not right. It shouldn't be this easy."*

"Yeah, I know."

"Can you see them? Can you tell how many are there?"

"I need to get closer."

"What's going on?" Logan whispers from beside me.

"The cats are asleep so we need to move fast."

Logan grips the doorknob leading to the basement and we both cringe when the hinges whine in response.

We instantly stop moving, stop breathing, and I take a moment to surf through the images in Stone's mind, but for some reason part of his thoughts are blocked. My stomach lurches because I know he's keeping something from me.

"I count at least a dozen cats," Stone says, *"But I have no idea if there are more."*

With no time to think about Stone's secrets, I peer into the basement and get my head back into the game. If we're up against a dozen cats, the odds aren't in our favor, but if we can free the seven members of Logan's family, then at least we stand a fighting chance. As I think about that an ominous shiver moves through me, and Logan puts his hand on my back.

"Remember what you promised me, Pride," he says.

I don't answer, instead I begin a slow descent. A second later I catch a very distinctive smell. I exchange a look with Logan before he hurries down the remaining stairs ahead of me and with my heart racing, I follow behind.

When we reach the bottom, Malcolm pushes off the cold cement floor, climbs to his feet, and grips the metal bar imprisoning him.

"Logan," he hurries out.

"It's okay, Malcolm," Logan says and checks the lock. "We're going to get you out of here."

Panic races through me as I watch the six other wolves jump at our voices and move in beside Malcolm in the packed cell.

I peer at the heavy lock. "Malcolm do you know where we can find a key?"

"Don't need one," Logan says and pulls what looks like two fingernail files from his back pocket. He grins. "Tricks of the trade. I stole them from your father's bathroom."

While Logan works the lock, I give each wolf a quick once over. When I see the metal collars on their necks, and see some sort of electric current running through them, dread takes hold of me because I know. I know how they're being controlled.

Electric shock.

But removing the collars will have to wait, because I need to get these wolves to safety before the cats awake. Feeling suddenly very anxious, I call out to Stone.

"*We found them. Logan is working the lock.*"

"*You'd better hurry. I think a few of the cats are stirring.*"

Hoping for an ally, I ask, "*Does Gem recognize the one she encountered?*"

He goes quiet for a moment then answers with, *"No. She doesn't see him."*

My heart jumps when the lock clicks open, and Logan pulls on the metal door to release the caged wolves.

Keeping my thoughts open to Stone, and without giving consideration to what he might find in my head, I gesture toward the stairs and step forward to take the lead. "We need to move. Fast."

I listen to joints groan in protest as I rush up the steps, and take a quick peek over my shoulder to see Logan herding them from behind, and realize that's just like Logan, always keeping watch over his pack. When we reach Stone, he ushers us all outside.

The cool night air breezes around us and we all remain silent as we quickly retrace our steps, but the second we turn the corner of the mansion, the world around us flips upside down and my heart leaps into my throat.

"Going somewhere?"

When I see the cruel face of a handler, his dark eyes brutal and unafraid, my wolf yelps and the sound prompts her into action.

Acting purely on instinct, I make a move toward him but don't miss the smug grin aimed my way. "I don't think so," he says, and when he pulls something from his pocket, something that reminds me of a tracking device, Malcolm and the others howl out loud and drop to their knees in excruciating pain. When I see a flickering blue glow flashing in the dark night I know they're being electrocuted.

Fury erupts inside me and I tear off my clothes, the sound of my bones crunching and grinding cutting through the night as my wolf takes shape. Just as I'm about to put a stop to his abuse once and for all, the handler's cats pounce out the door behind us, awakened by the tortured howls echoing off the distant mountains.

I look at the collars around their black necks, and can only assume they're controlled by a different device. If only I could get my hands on it. I take a moment to consider the odds and even though they don't stack up in our favor, there isn't one wolf among us about to tuck tail and run.

The wolves who've travelled to the compound with me take that moment to shift, joining me in animal form. I hear Officer Sanford draw his gun, but as the sleek black cats form a wide berth around us, protecting their master, he's unable to get a clear shot. He also knows better than to waste a bullet on a panther just yet.

Everything inside me tightens because I know this fight can only end in bloodshed, and only one species will be walking out of here today.

A movement from my peripheral vision gains my attention, and my wolf reacts to danger a second before I do. This time I don't stop her, because this time I heed my father's advice and understand she has to do whatever it takes to protect her family. And nothing, not even me, can hold her back from doing it.

When light floods the area, sharp teeth flare and green cat eyes glisten beneath the illumination as it pounces. With an attack well underway I hear Sanford's gun ring out. But I can't think about who's been shot, because I'm about to be hit. In a movement that takes the panther by surprise, I dodge the stealthy animal seconds before it lands on me. I hit the ground hard and the sweet smell of autumn grass fills my senses as I roll across the manicured lawns to gain purchase. I jump to my feet, my long nails piercing the soil as I watch the other wolves in my pack face their own attackers.

All around me I hear growls and whines as dog faces cat. Deep in the shadows where the floodlight can't quite reach, I catch a glimpse of Officer Sanford as he goes after the handler, gun drawn and aimed at the man's back.

Somewhere in the distance a gunshot rings out and there is a small part of me that registers the sound, registers that it's not from Sanford's gun. But my brain is too preoccupied with the fight to comprehend what that means.

The cat climbs to its feet and shakes the daze from its head but I don't give it time to fully clear its rattled brain. I jump through the air and land on top of it with a thud. It bares its teeth in retaliation and when its sharp nails claw my fur and slice my flesh wide open, I go for its jugular. I clamp down but before I can draw blood I'm attacked from behind.

I'm tossed through the air like a tattered rag doll, the world around me spinning out of control, but I manage to land on my feet and when I do, I let loose a thunderous growl, my wolf preparing her counter attack.

Looking hard and feral, both cats circle me, and I use that moment to assess the situation. Drawing on everything Logan taught me while we were hunting in Olympic Park, I take in their stance, and when I notice the position of their back legs, I know they're preparing to pounce. And I know what I have to do. My wolf crouches low, waiting for the perfect moment to make her move.

That's when I hear Stone's distressed howl. I spare him a glance and darkness churns in his eyes seconds before he turns from me and tears the head clear of the cat he's battling with. Blood spills across the grass and rouses the hunger in the courtyard.

From my peripheral vision I catch a glimpse of another vicious panther headed Stone's way, but he rushes to my aid instead of fighting. The second he moves from the cat's line of sight, it turns its attention to Gem, who is already backed up against the wall and outnumbered.

"Stone, no!" I cry out. *"I've got this."* But he keeps coming my way, his single minded focus to save me at everyone else's expense clearly placing Gem in danger.

My cry gains Logan's attention. He lifts his head from the cat he killed and a split second later he's flying through the air. His growl is fierce, his look dangerous. A moment later he's jumping, and pivoting off the side of the house to barrel toward the string of cats about to tear into Gem. When Logan hits with the power of a speeding truck, they all tumble like bowling pins and he's able to pull Gem to safety.

A cry of relief crawls from my throat and from the distance another shot rings out. That's when real fear hits because I instantly know what's going on.

The scouts have arrived.

Stone intercepts the cats aimed my way, and when a third enters the fight, I know I have to do something. I try to go for him but a shot punctures the ground in front of me. When the bullet pummels the earth, dirt flies up to meet my face and I crouch low. My father comes toward me, his muzzle awash with blood and the scent of his breath is so foul it turns my stomach

A forth cat joins the fight against Stone, and when his cries echo around me, I make another move to go, but the gunfire coming from the mountain halts my motion. My brain races and my pulse beats against my throat like mad. I have to do something but if I step into the line of fire I'll surely get shot and then won't be of any use to anyone.

Before I know what's happening, Logan is running at breakneck speed, his wolf so swift his image blurs as he rushes by. I blink against the hurried flash and time seems to stand still as he moves with purpose, his powerful claws and fangs tearing the panthers off Stone and sending them flying through the air one by one, saving Stone from imminent death.

With his body a battered mess and his fur coated in blood, Stone climbs to all fours. A second later the two alphas stand side by side, and the combination of power as they join forces is enough to make my wolf howl. As they form an alliance to combat our enemy I know in a battle of life and death nothing or no one can stand a chance against these two wolves.

The second I hear another zing of a bullet I duck, and when it flies past my face, parting my hair on the side, my wolf growls.

Knowing Gem is safe, and Logan and Stone have things under control, I duck behind a bush and consider the angle of the shot. I quickly shift back to human, grab my gun off the pile of clothes I discarded earlier and shoot for a tree on the south side of the mountain. That's when I see the PTF Officer turn in the direction of my bullet. That moment of inattention is all I need. I rush toward the metal fence, shifting back to wolf as I jump it, and using my exceptional speed I rush up the mountain and pounce.

The PTF officer lands with a hard thud, and frantically yells for backup as he grips my ruff and tries to wrestle me off. But I'm too strong. I know it, and from the horrified look in his eyes, he knows it too.

I snarl at him, and his face goes pale. Then, with every intention of debilitating him, I clamp my jowls around his neck and puncture his skin. Since my goal is to slow him down, not kill him—I still hold out hope that I can prove we're not all monsters—I purposely miss his jugular.

When fresh blood saturates the air, I life my muzzle and howl at the black sky. Knowing this man no longer poses an immediate threat to those I call family, I climb off his body and leave him to his own fate.

But when I turn and come face to face with another officer, and find a gun pointed directly at my head the world around me slows to a crawl.

The minute I look into his hard eyes I realize how naïve and foolish I've been, because from everything in the way those brutal eyes are glaring down at me I know there is nothing I can to do convince him all wolves aren't monsters.

This is a war I can't possibly win.

As I stare down the barrel of a gun my life flashes before me, and I think about the remorse I spotted in my father's eyes the night we were outside the mountain den. At the time I thought it was because of something he'd lost, or something he was going to lose. But I now understand the remorse lingering below the surface was for me and what I was going to lose.

Hope for a normal life.

He knew it could never happen. Knew I could never change the minds of so many. Knew I'd have to keep the wolf side of me alive and remain in kill or be kill mode if I wanted to survive in this harsh world.

When I hear the pin drop, I make a move to bolt, even though I know I can't outrun a silver bullet. But since my survival instincts are strong and it's not in my nature to go down without a fight, I dig my nails into the ground to gain leverage.

As the bullet engages and speeds toward me I howl, and in the instant before I move, I'm shoved to the ground, my head hitting hard against a rock. Pushing through the pain and nausea, I hear the bullet hit flesh, hear the howl of an injured wolf before it drops to the ground in the spot I was just standing, taking the hit that was meant to be mine.

"*No!*" I yell when I see my father roll down the hill, leaving a thick trail of blood in his wake. The world around me goes into slow motion and I jump up, knock the officer to the ground, and swipe at his neck with my long, deadly talons. As he gasps for breath, I leave him to his own fate and rush after my father.

He tumbles down the hill and lands with a hard thud

against the side of the gate. I hurry to him, my head spinning and my stomach in knots.

I look at the puncture wound and watch the flesh around the opening turn black, and there is nothing I can do to stop the bleeding, nothing I can do to keep the poison from invading his body. I go down on my haunches and push at him with my muzzle.

"*Papa,*" I cry frantically.

"*Pride,*" he says, and his voice is so low and so strained I can barely hear him.

"*Papa, please...*"

"*I never meant to hurt you,*" he says.

"*I know,*" I manage past the lump in my throat. And I really do know. He only ever meant to protect me, and he did it the best way he knew how.

His tongue flicks out to wet his mouth and I can tell he's losing his fight to speak. "*I hope someday you'll forgive me,*" he murmurs.

"*I do,*" I say and think about how Logan once told me that someday soon I'd learn all about forgiveness, because forgiveness is about love, and this man really does love me. "*I do forgive you. Please, don't die. You can't leave me. Not now.*"

"*I have to go Pride. I've had to go for quite some time now. I'm just glad I got to know you first.*" As soon as the words leave his mouth understanding rolls through me.

He's dying.

The foul smell I've noticed coming from his breath is the scent of death. Since I've been imprisoned my whole life, I've never known a wolf to die of old age or natural causes before and had no way to identify the sour aroma. But Logan knew, and he wanted to protect me from it for as long as he could. He knew I had to learn about love and forgiveness and find my place in this world before I could deal with the harsh reality of my father's fate.

"*I forgive you, Papa,*" I say again, and when I put my paw over his, all the answers fall into place. Staring down the face of death is what prompted him to change his life around. It made him want to right all his wrongs.

"*I'm going to go be with your mother now,*" he says, and attempts a smile before saying, "*I hope she can find it in her heart to forgive me, too.*" With that he exhales his very last breath and my heart clenches so hard, the pain cuts through my body like a serrated knife.

When I feel the life leave him and he returns to his human form, a big hiccupping sob crawls out of my throat and reverberates off the mountain. Through watery eyes I look beyond the gate to see Logan rushing toward me. He sidesteps all the dead panthers and his big paws turn red as they sink into the blood soaked grass.

"*Pride,*" he says and comes closer, the look in his pewter eyes sad, mournful, but seconds before he reaches the gate, a vicious cat jumps the fence from behind me and clamps down on his jugular.

Logan puts up a hard fight but there isn't much he can do as the cat gives a savage shake of its head and tears into his throat. I can hear the cords on his neck popping and when sharp canines sink in deeper, Logan's powerful, streamlined body drops to the ground. The warm scent of fresh blood sprays my face and fills the night air.

"*No!*"

It takes less than a split second for me to understand the boy I mated with is going to die if I don't do something. As that reality hits, I let my wolf off her leash. I might not be an assassin any longer, but my wolf knows what she has to do.

Before anyone can react, I jump the fence and rush the powerful cat, and when it turns sharp teeth on me and bites through my shoulder a scream lodges in my throat. With everything happening so fast, my brain can barely keep up. I feel like a bystander watching my wolf as she lets her rage power her attack and knock the cat clear off Logan's body.

The panther flies backwards and I immediately do the one thing Logan asked me not to. I purposely position myself between Logan and the cat, putting myself in the direct line of fire.

The cat hisses at me, and knowing I have to call on everything Logan taught me about survival, I face this instinct-driven cat using both my heart and my head. I taunt it, pretending it's no threat by going down on my haunches to groom myself.

Reacting like I knew it would, it pounces and flies through the air at me, and because my wolf is small she's able to slide under its airborne body, and the cat slams to the ground behind me with an audible thud.

I catch Stone rushing my way, but knowing this is my fight, I spin around before he can reach me, before the cat can gain purchase. With all my strength, I grab its head and rip it clear off its shoulders.

When its body goes limp, no longer able to hurt the boy I mated with, I hear someone shout, "*Stop!*"

13

"*Stop!*"

When that one word rings in my ears, my wolf registers the meaning and I glance up to see a boy coming close. From his thick, dark hair and rich cognac coloring, I know he's a shifter.

A panther in a boy's body!

I growl low and prepare to make short work of him, so I can attend to Logan, knowing he's going to die on me if I don't, but Gem jumps up from her crouched position near the house. She yells at me but with my wolf in kill mode, I give a savage shake of my head to warn her away.

"*No, Pride. This is the boy who helped me,*" she says and quickly turns back to her human form. That's when I see Officer Sanford coming from around the house, and watch Malcolm and the others climb to their feet, their collars now deactivated. I exchange a look with Officer Sanford, and when I meet his eyes, I know the handler, and every panther except the one standing next to Gem is dead.

With that I turn my back to the crowd and crawl toward Logan, my heart aching painfully.

"*Please, Logan,*" I cry, unable to keep the desperation from my voice. "*You have to shift and heal yourself. I can't lose you. I can't.*" But as I plead with him, I wonder if he's too far gone, too weak to shift.

After a long agonizing moment, his eyes flicker open, and his breath is labored when he says, "*You broke your promise.*"

"*What are you talking about?*" I hurry out, trying to keep the panic at bay as I watch blood gush from his neck. I put my paw over the wound, but there is nothing I can do to seal the gash.

"*You said you wouldn't put yourself in danger because of me.*"

"*Logan,*" I cry out. "*You know I'm not about to stand by and watch you die.*"

He nudges me with his muzzle and pewter eyes narrow as his voice goes serious. "*But you promised and mates aren't supposed to lie to each other, Pride.*"

I gulp air as his silver orbs move over mine, and I don't miss the way he calls us mates, don't miss the implication in what he's saying, what he's asking.

"*Please Logan, you have to shift. I need you.*"

"*I know you need me, Pride. I need you, too. But the thing is, I don't just want to be the one you need, I want to be the one you want.*"

I exhale a long, slow breath and with my emotions in complete turmoil I can't stop myself from blurting out, "*Logan, you* are *the one I want. You're the one I've always wanted and always needed. Don't you see, it's always been you. Always.*"

With that Logan shifts, and as I watch the wound on his neck heal, and realize the cat only grazed his jugular, I quickly return to my human form. Ignoring those around us we rush to each other and cling like our lives depend on it, and somewhere in the back of my mind, I realize they do. The voices in the courtyard fade to a distant buzz as we hold each other, drawing strength, courage and love from our tight embrace.

His scent seeps under my skin and pulls a howl from my

wolf. I grip him harder, my fingernails biting into his skin while tears spill down my face. We stay like that for an endless minute and I let my wolf take comfort in his protective arms, let her give herself over to this boy completely, body, heart and soul.

After a long while, Logan pushes my hair off my face and says, "It's going to be okay, Pride. It's all over."

Gem steps up to us and hands us our clothes. Logan and I stay close, our bodies constantly touching as we dress, and while I feel Stone surfing the outer edges of my thoughts, I can't quite bring myself to look at him, can't quite deal with his emotions when mine are so out of control.

In need of a distraction while I get myself in check, I drag my shirt over my head and look at all the spilled blood, all the senseless death and destruction, then turn to take one last glance at the body of my father.

With my heart aching for those I've loved and lost, every single thing my father said to me over the last week resonates in my mind. He knew I had to go down a dark, dangerous road before figuring out I could never change mankind. Our species will always be hunted. The best we can do in this harsh world is to find a way to survive and work to define our *normal*.

Thinking of normal has me thinking of Officer Sanford and how he needs our help to determine which wolves are rogues and which can be saving. Logan might have just told me it was over, but I know it will never be over. Not for me.

It's true that I want to stop fighting, especially since someday I want to start a family with Logan, but how can I walk away from this war? How can I turn my back on those that need me? As soon as that thought enters my head, Stone steps up to me.

"Pride," he says, and there is nothing he can do to mask his emotions from me.

I look into his tortured eyes, hating how lost he is, and when I think about what he heard me say to Logan, and think about how much that must have hurt him, sadness swells in my chest, squeezing to the point of pain.

"Stone," I choke out, having no idea where to begin. I reach out to him, expecting to find anger and sorrow, but the strange, unfamiliar energy I discover instead catches me off guard and has my wolf wailing.

Intense eyes full of deep understanding watch me for a long time and I feel him in my head soothing my worries before he finally breaks the mounting tension and announces, "It is over for you, Pride. It's time for you to walk away from this."

"What are you talking about?"

He briefly looks at Logan. "You've found your path, and now it's my turn to find mine."

My throat aches painfully as heartache sets my chest on fire and that's when I realize he'd been in my head earlier, and knew my choice long before this moment.

"Stone—"

"Your fight is over, Pride. I want you to travel to the Jasper Mountains with Logan and his family so you can make the home you always wanted. I want you to live a normal life."

"Stone, no," I cry out.

He steps closer, his heat reaching out to me. "No, Pride. It's what I want for you. All I ever wanted was to keep you safe, you know that. And the only way I can ensure you remain unharmed is if I hit the streets with Sanford. That way I can protect you from the outside."

"What are you saying?" I ask, my rattled brain racing to catch up.

"I'm going to help him hunt, and I'm going to help him rescue kids like Blaze." I stare at him and that's when I know why he blocked a portion of his thoughts from me. He knew how this was going to end, knew I wasn't going like the dangerous path he's chosen.

But how can I stop him when he's so desperately trying to find his way? I swallow, and when I think about his strength of character, the incredible kindness inside him, my words lodge in my throat.

"Besides, Nova is still out there and I can't take the chance she'll come after you."

I open my mouth, but he cuts me off and says, "Don't worry. I won't kill her." He shrugs, "I guess on some twisted level I can understand why she did what she did. Love really can make a person act crazy." He pauses, then adds, "I think she's trying to find her way every bit as much as I am and you never know, maybe I can convince her to hunt with me."

I grip his shirt and hold him tight, hardly able to believe what he's saying, hardly able to believe he's no longer going to be in my life.

His face softens and he brushes his finger over my cheek. He stares at me for a long time before saying, "I once told you that I could never let you walk away from me again, that it would kill me. But I want you to know I'm going to be okay, because this time, Pride, I'm the one who's walking away from you."

A cry lodges in my throat as I listen and digest what he's telling me. When I think about him leaving my mind races back to my father's mansion, to the time he paired Stone with Officer Sanford. That's when it hits me. My father knew. He knew what he was doing when he matched Stone and the former PTF officer. He knew all along where I belonged, and knew those two had a greater purpose. He was forging alliances, building trust and bonds, because my future and the future of our kind depend on them.

Stone turns to Logan. "I was wrong about you," he says. "You're more than capable of taking care of her." His eyes flicker to Gem. "And everyone else." As I watch him, watch the hate leave his eyes, I understand how heroic and courageous he really is. When a small strained smile turns up the corner of his mouth, I know an uneasy truce has been made between the two most amazing guys in my life.

My throat closes over, tears spilling harder now.

Stone turns back to me, his dark eyes swimming with raw emotions. "If it were anyone else, I'd never let you go, Pride."

I choke and cling to him. Stone holds me for a moment, then grips my shoulders. He eases back, and I feel Logan's strong arm slip around my waist.

The two alphas stand eye to eye, then Stone puts his hand on Logan's shoulder. As they stare at each other Stone says, "Take good care of her."

Logan places his hand on Stone's shoulder. "You know I will."

With that Stone backs up and gives a slow nod. "I do."

"Take care of yourself, Stone."

Stone's glance goes from Logan to me and he says, "Take care of each other." He turns back to Logan. "Get her out of here, Sanford and I will take care of this mess."

With that he turns from us and I stare at his retreating back as he walks toward Officer Sanford. My heart lurches while I watch him go. I reach out to him mentally, to say one last goodbye. To say what I should have said to him a long time ago. Thank you.

"*Stone*," I yell and run toward him.

His movements still and he angles his head unnaturally, but when my call to him goes unanswered, I suck in a sharp breath and wonder what's going on.

"*Stone*," I cry again, almost frantic as I search for him in the dark.

"*Hey*," I hear, and spin so fast I nearly lose my balance.

"*Logan?*"

His smile is slow, and the warmth in his eyes runs so deep it washes over my soul and brings a new kind of heat to my body. "*Yeah, Pride. It's me.*"

"*Logan,*" I say my heart racing in confusion. "*You're in my head. How? Why?*"

But then I remember what my father once said. Sometimes bonds are tested, broken even. And it's only then that new, deeper connections can be made.

"*Come here,*" he says.

I rush to him and he circles his hands around my waist to lift me clear off the ground. Warm lips settle over mine and he whispers into my mouth. "It's time for us to go find our normal, Pride. Your fight is over."

Sheer exhaustion takes hold and my lids fight to close as Logan drives the overstuffed SUV back to my father's house. From the passenger seat I angle my head to see him, and when he offers me a warm smile full of love and kindness, my heart squeezes in my chest.

He holds my hand and I blink to keep my eyes open as I listen to Malcolm question the panther that once spared Gem. When I learn of the atrocities committed against their kind, I understand that when it comes right down to it, these panthers are just as innocent in all this as we are—used as pawns in a world where greed rules.

The boy goes on to explain that he wasn't from the primitive village that the other shifters had come from. He'd merely been captured in the crossfire. And unlike his pride in the African jungle, where the human part of them knows the difference between right and wrong, there are still many cat colonies out there that run on pure on instinct. Just like there are some wolves out there who always let their primal side rule.

He has no idea how they were first found and recognized

as shifters by men in America, and doesn't suppose he'll ever know. All he knows is he wants to keep the others in his pride safe, and the best way he knows how is by staying on American soil and stopping the hunters before they set out to trap another.

As I think about that, and all that has happened over the last month, my lids slip shut. With Logan beside me, keeping watch over me, I allow myself to drift off until we reach my father's estate.

Once we're sure there are no other panthers stalking the compound, we make our way up the winding path. With the plan to spend one more night here to rest up before we take off to Richmond's Village in the Jasper Mountains, we all climb from the car. Once inside the house, I talk quietly to the guards about my father as everyone makes their way to their rooms.

After speaking with the guards, I walk to the kitchen while the others prepare for bed. That's when I see a manila envelope on the table, addressed to me.

My pulse leaps as I pick it up. I carefully peel it open and when I glance inside to see a stack of pictures, emotions bombard me, because deep in my heart I know. I know my father left this because he never expected to come back.

Logan steps up behind me, "You okay?"

"I'm okay," I answer and while I can't bear to look at the photos, there is a part of me that takes great comfort in knowing my father was watching over me all these years, the best way he knew how.

I draw in a breath, and when I pull in the estate's aroma and a different, yet familiar scent fills my senses, a new calmness comes over me. As Logan stands with his back to my chest, and my skin begins to prickle, I know my fight is not quite over.

I put the envelope down, and turn to Logan. "I need to be

alone for a minute, okay?" While it's not a lie, it's not entirely true either. But I need him to walk away, because the fight I'm about to face is my fight and mine alone.

Logan hesitates for a moment, and I feel tension ripple through his body. "Okay," he says, and when he steps away, a chill moves through me, partly from the loss of his heat, and partly from the scent that is souring my stomach.

I feel Logan hovering on the outer edges of my thoughts. He's an alpha. A protector. I know it's not easy for him to step back and let me do what I have to do, but I love the faith he has in my abilities, and love even more that while he's walked away, he's still staying close.

With movements that are swift and purposeful, I head straight to the kitchen drawer, and pull it open. When I find what I'm looking for, what I'd discovered days earlier, I spin around and come face to face with the man from my nightmares.

"Pride," he greets me, flecks of pewter puncturing his cruel eyes. Then he gives me a brutal grin and I watch his bones shift, his body preparing to morph, to kill the young pup who has given him nothing but trouble. "I should have known I could never take you by surprise."

"Why?" I ask, my voice hard, my wolf waiting for the signal, but I don't need my wolf for this battle. No. The girl in me is going to take this fight on. "Why did you force Sandy to change you?"

He grunts deep in his throat. "Come on, Pride. You're smarter than that."

I stare at his face and note how much he's aged over the last few weeks and the sight of his tired eyes has me thinking of my father. That's when the pieces of the puzzle come together. "You were sick," I say. "You were dying."

His grin is dark, menacing. "And now I'm not."

"We can get sick and die, just like humans," I challenge.

"Wolves live for centuries before old age kicks in, and with these new regenerative abilities, I'm as healthy as ever." Looking a bit bored by the whole conversation he says, "Okay, let's make this quick, shall we. I have things to do, and a few wolves to claim."

When his eyes meet mine, I know what he's thinking, that he's more powerful than me now, and while I know better than to ever underestimate him, I know he's still underestimating me.

That's his first mistake.

I hold my ground. "Of course, old age and sickness isn't the only way wolves can die. You of all people know that."

Eyes unafraid as they stare at me, he lets loose a bark of laughter, and I know he sees me as no challenge. But when I take my hand out from behind my back, and he sees what I have, his laughter dies an abrupt death. I keep my wolf settled as he drops to the floor and calls on his wolf.

That's his second mistake.

Because before he can complete his transformation, I rush at him and knowing I never should have left anything to chance, never should have assumed those panthers had killed him, I do the one thing I should have done in the first place.

I slap a collar around his neck.

His bark echoes off the walls around me, but his tortured cries are short lived. Because he's too inexperienced to know how to leash his wild side in the midst of transformation, and there is nothing he can do to halt the shift from man to wolf, nothing he can do to prevent the collar from snapping his neck.

As I look at him, I let loose a long, piercing howl and think of all those I've loved and lost, all those who were tortured and abused by his hands.

All those I vowed to avenge.

I take in the unnatural angle of his head, and know in my heart that justice has finally been served.

When I look up and see Logan in the doorway, his body, heart and soul reaching out to me, I draw a deep breath, let it out ever so slowly and say, "Now it's over."

EPILOGUE

F ive years later.
    Pacific Ocean

I squish the glorious white sand between my toes, my body completely warm and content as I blink against the bright sun glistening on the pacific waters. Logan waves to me from the shore, then leans down to grab the small chubby hand reaching up for him.

Using slow, careful steps they move toward me. As I watch them, my heart gives a little putter against my chest, and I grab my camera from my bag to take a picture of two of the most important people in my life.

Water drips from Logan's beautiful, athletic body as he tosses the little blonde bundle of energy over his shoulder. He looks back at me and his smile is warm and tender when I snap the picture. I twist to put the camera away, and when I open the bag and see the stack of pictures that have been sitting there in a manila envelope untouched for five long years, I draw a deep breath, deciding today is the day. It's time to finally face the past, and keep good on the promise I once made, one I was never sure I could keep. My shoulders stiffen, and I blow out a long slow breath as a riot of emotions moves through me.

"*Hey*," Logan says when he picks up on my anxiety, speaking to me telepathically so the astute little bundle on his shoulders isn't privy to my worries. His eyes narrow in concern. "*Everything okay?*"

I pat the blanket beside me. "Come sit down," I say to him. After removing sweet little Abigail Stone from his shoulders, named after the woman who gave birth to me, and one of the alphas responsible for my life today, Logan drops down onto the blanket.

The most beautiful two year old in the world settles herself on my lap, and I hand her a juice box while I dig out the pictures.

Logan smiles at me, and brushes my hair from my shoulders. "You sure?"

I nod. "It's time."

"Momma." Bright blue eyes that remind me of the ocean —remind me of freedom—blink up at me.

"Look Abby," I say and show her the picture of me when I wasn't much older than her.

"Abby," she says and I smile because, except for having her father's eyes, the similarities between mother and daughter are uncanny.

"No, it's momma," I correct.

"Momma," she repeats.

We flip through a few more pictures until I come across one where I'm standing on my father's lawn at his California mansion. It was the day we stood outside and scented the panthers, the same day my father pulled grass from my hair. I think back to that moment and remember when he walked away, saying he had some last minute things to take care of. This is what he'd been up to, pulling and printing images from the security camera.

When I consider the rest of the horrible events of that day, I remember what he asked of me, and all he taught me in the short time we managed to spend together. There was a purpose to his every action, a reason for his every word. And that purpose was to prepare me.

As my heart races faster, emotions bombard me and I continue to flip through the pile. The next picture is another one of us standing together. It was only later that day that I knew why he wanted a photo of us together, united. He wanted to leave me with at least one good memory before he died.

I think about his death. All the senseless deaths from that day. I'm not proud of the killing I did. I never wanted to be an assassin. But I had to protect my family, had to let my wolf do what she needed to. Like my father once told me I would. Like he did for me.

I think about Stone, and what he, too, did for me. I used to feel him watching, but no longer do. I can only hope he's found his path and that some girl will love him as much as I do. When I think about the kind of girl he needs, it brings a smile to my face. I know true love will happen for him one day and I also know it will be one heck of a roller coaster ride when it does.

Pulling my thoughts back, I point to my father in the picture. "This is your grand-papa."

As I think about what my father asked of me tears cling to my lashes, and I can feel Logan inside my head, there to support me. Always there to pick me up when I've fallen down.

"Abby," I begin, then go quiet for a minute, remembering how Logan once told me love was about forgiveness. "We've all made mistakes at one time or another. But he really loved me. Just like your papa and your momma really love you."

"Papa," she says this time.

I tip her chin until she's looking up at me. "And your grand-papa would have loved you, too, Abby."

Abby points a chubby finger at the picture, and says, "Grand-papa."

I look past her shoulder and as I stare at the ocean I think back to five years ago when I set out on a journey to change the world so I could live a normal life. At the time I thought normal meant going to school, hanging at the mall, wearing fashionable clothes, and suppressing the primal side of me until each shift night.

I quickly learned that wasn't my normal, and never would be. My father tried to teach me that. To prepare me for the world and to warn that if I lose my wolf, I lose the purpose of my life.

The purpose of a shifter, which is much different from the purpose of a human, is to survive, to find happiness and to protect our packs in a world that wants us all dead. In order to do that we must learn from the elders and pass on our knowledge to the youth. My father forgot his purpose, and before he died he wanted to make sure I knew mine. He followed me back to California, to confront the PTF, so I could learn those hard truths myself.

What I learned was that my purpose isn't about going to school, working alongside humans while pretending we're no different. Because the truth is we are different, and while I know humans will never accept us, I also understand our differences aren't a bad thing. It's those differences that make me who I am today, and thanks to three very important men in my life, I like the person I've become.

I once thought I wanted to be more human than wolf, to let that side of me die and only come out on shift night. But I was wrong. My father taught me that I can never forget the primal side of me. He was right.

I can't allow the human side, or even the wolf side to ever overpower the other. It's only when a happy medium is met, when I embrace and accept both sides equally that I can serve my purpose, and look to my future.

The future of my family.

Logan's pack knew that. While they went to school, were productive members of society, and took to the woods on shift nights, they never once forgot who they were. I always thought they suppressed their primal side in order to become more human, but I was wrong about that. I was wrong about a lot of things.

But I was right about a lot of things, too.

Logan takes Abby off my lap, and pulls her to him, then he drags me into a three way embrace. As Abby spills her juice all over us and squirms her way out we both laugh, because we both know that she's so much like me and is undoubtedly going to grow up to be a handful.

Logan's pacific blue eyes meet mine, and my chest clenches so tightly with the love I feel for him, that I can barely fill my lungs. While I might not have lived the life of a typical teenager, when I look at my mate, my daughter, and think about all the things we've yet to learn, yet to teach, I know *this* is my normal, and I wouldn't change it for the world.

AFTERWORD

Thank You!

Thank you so much for reading Pride's Pursuit, book three in my Pride series. I hope you enjoyed the story as much as I loved writing it. Read on for an excerpt of Crashing Down, book one in my Stone Cliff series.

Interested in leaving a review? Please do! Reviews help readers connect with books that work for them. I appreciate all reviews, whether positive or negative.

Happy Reading,
   Cathryn

CRASHING DOWN

"You reek of sex."

Noah Ryan grinned at his buddy Jared, a guy he'd gotten to know over the last couple of years while living and working at Stone Cliff Resort in the Canadian Rocky Mountains. Taking his friend's ribbing in stride, Noah scrubbed his hands through his disheveled hair, and sank down onto the driftwood next to him, setting his motorcycle helmet at his feet. He let his glance surf over the crowd gathered around the nightly, beachside bonfire. He zeroed in on a cute blonde with big tits and gave Jared a wry smirk. "Not yet I don't."

Jared reached into the cooler, pulled out a cold brew, and handed it to Noah. "Yeah, well that's a matter of opinion."

"Fuck you." Noah laughed and twisted off the cap, the taste of weed and smoke scratching his dry throat like coarse sandpaper. "How the hell can I reek of sex when I just crawled out of bed, *alone*?"

Jared shrugged. "Well your bed smells like sex, then."

Okay, so that was probably true. His bed likely did smell like sex. Sometimes a hard, mindless fuck chased away the chills that had taken up residency inside him since the accident a little over three years ago. Then again, sometimes it didn't. Sometimes the demons managed to tunnel their way past the wall he'd built despite a warm body lying next to him.

Noah took a long pull from the bottle, and washed the grit from his throat. Too bad the alcohol did little to drown the pain that blackened his soul. Then again, did he really deserve for it to?

He worked to push all dark thoughts aside, and tried to keep things light. He nudged his friend with his elbow. "Ah, come on, Jared. Don't be jealous 'cause I'm getting all the play and you're not."

Jared waved to Ryan and Bobbie, a couple of locals who had just rolled in, before he flicked his beer cap at Noah. "Yeah, well, fuck you. I get all the play I need, or I would be if you weren't always hovering around." Two well-built, dark-haired hotties moved in front of them, smiling flirtatiously at Noah. "Christ, Noah, what the hell is it about you?" He clucked his tongue and added, "You're like nectar to the honey bee, my man."

Laughing, Noah took another swig from the bottle as the cute blonde he'd been eying glanced his way. He caught the mischief in her gaze and pegged her as a local, a rich townie who'd just returned home from university. He knew her type all too well. She'd spend her days lounging on the water with her friends and her nights here at the beach, otherwise known as the Cave, where many of the resort staff and locals alike gathered for a little action. Not that he was judging her. He wasn't. After all, unlike him she was getting an education and going places.

With exhaustion pulling at him, Noah stretched his arms over his head and stifled a yawn. He hadn't planned on hanging out with Jared tonight, but since he couldn't take staring at his ceiling for one more minute, he'd decided if he couldn't sleep, he might as well get laid. The little townie gave him a look that said, *come get some* and his cock twitched, but before he made his move on the blonde, he shifted closer to his friend. He pulled an envelope from his back pocket and slipped it to him, wanting to do this exchange off resort and away from their manager, Donald Brake's, watchful eye.

"Noah…" Jared looked down at the envelope and shook his head. "Shit." He stole a quick glance around before he shoved the bills into his pocket. "But you were saving…you can't afford—"

"And you can't afford not to." He looked pointedly at the swelling beneath Jared's bruised eye. Even though he claimed the injury had happened when he fell off the raft during yesterday's rough, white-water ride down Canyon Run, Noah knew better. Noah pitched his voice low, his words for Jared's ears only. "You keep fucking with these guys and you'll lose more than just your job. You know that, right?"

"Yeah, yeah, I know," Jared said gravely, dark eyes cast downward in worry as he rubbed his temples with his thumbs. "Christ, I had a straight flush. I never thought I could lose." He fisted his short-cropped hair and gave a tug. "I mean come on, what are the fucking odds that the other guy beat me with a royal flush?"

"A trillion to one," Noah said. He didn't need to do the mental math that came so easily to him as he finished off his beer and reached for another, handing one to Jared as well. Even though Jared was as big a fuck up as he was, the guy was a damn hard worker, and in a few short years had climbed his way up from bellboy to concierge. That job was his life, and Noah wasn't about to stand around and see it get taken from him.

It was Jared's job to get to know the guests and see that their needs were being met. What he wasn't supposed to do was socialize with those guests, or get himself invited to the after-hours poker game that the resort's management turned a blind eye to. The high-rolling businessmen, who came to town for the annual weeklong event, weren't the kind of guys who took kindly to getting stiffed. You owed them money, you paid your debt. One way or another.

Noah's glance shot to the blonde. Then again, who was he too lecture about rules, considering he was about to break one himself? Even when off duty, the staff wasn't supposed to do anything to bring negative attention to the resort, which meant that picking up a local for a quick fuck on the rocks was pretty much all kinds of wrong.

"I'll pay you back," Jared said.

The blonde gave Noah a once over and a satisfied grin. "You just keep yourself out of trouble."

Jared followed the direction of Noah's gaze, and when he glimpsed the girl Noah had his sights set on, he shook his head. "You're one to talk. That girl has trouble written all over her."

"Good," Noah said, smirking.

"She's got a boyfriend, Noah," Jared warned. "And he's a big bastard."

"I think you're mistaken." Ignoring Jared's warning, Noah stood and shoved one hand into his pocket, pulling his worn and faded jeans lower on his hips, a not so subtle invitation that brought the blonde's attention right where he wanted it. "I think she's looking for a little play."

Jared gave him a look that suggested he was either crazy, or had a death wish, or possibly both. Maybe he was right.

"Yeah? What makes you say that?" Jared asked.

"She wouldn't be wearing a shirt that showed off her tits if she didn't want me to look."

While Jared cursed under his breath, Noah moved through the throng of people. Seconds before he reached blondie, some douche bag stepped in front of him to block his path. Noah nudged him with his shoulder, shoving him out of the way. With single-minded determination he moved past him, but when the guy said, "Is there a problem here, pal?" it stopped Noah dead in his tracks.

He turned and sized up the steroid-induced mouth breather and shrugged. "Listen dude," Noah began. "As far as I can tell the only problem here is that you're standing between me," he paused to poke his finger in the direction of the girl watching him with big, curious eyes, "and her."

The guy grabbed Noah's arm, his nostrils flaring as he yanked Noah closer. Even at six feet, Noah had to lift his chin to meet the guy's eyes. The ogre gripped him tighter, his sausage fingers digging into Noah's biceps.

Like a wire stretched tight, Noah snapped. "Get the fuck off me." His skin came alive as he jerked his arm free. Christ, he didn't like to be touched. Touching made him feel...well, it made him *feel*.

Old, blood-soaked memories clawed their way to the surface, and visions of his best friend clutching his arm like it was his lifeline swamped him. But Noah hadn't been Jonny's lifeline. Oh no, not at all. Noah was a fuck up, and the sole reason Jonny was dead.

"...Noah."

He heard Jared saying something, pleading with him, but the words were lost in the foggy haze clouding his mind, riding circles around his brain on the pain that came with remembering.

"Maybe you should listen to your boyfriend," the ogre said.

Noah laughed in his face. "Maybe you should suck my dick."

The mouth breather fisted his hands and drew his arm

back. Heart racing, Noah stood there, his body braced as he prepared for the pain. Welcomed it.

Deserved it.

Like a hard fuck, sometimes a good punch in the face sent the demons scurrying. For a little while, anyway.

The hit came sure and swift, and Noah's teeth clashed as he flew backwards toward the water. The damp sandy shore padded his fall, but the cold waves crashing over his body snapped his groggy senses back to life faster than a broken condom. He jumped to his feet and spit a mouth full of blood onto the sand as the primate came at him again, his knuckles practically dragging on the ground.

"Stop it, Alex," a shrill voice cried out, and Noah's heart sank as the girl he'd been stalking halted the fight. Jesus, he'd wanted that next blow. Craved it. Noah wiped his mouth with the back of his hand as blondie pounded her fists into Alex's chest.

Fuck if Jared hadn't been right. Blondie did have a boyfriend, and the big bastard's name was Alex.

Alex grabbed the girl's hands, and pinned them to her sides. She squirmed and fought against him, the back of her shirt lifting to show a tramp stamp that Noah was certain her good folks knew nothing about. Damned if she wasn't just the girl he needed tonight.

"Stay out of this, Dara," the ape named Alex warned.

Noah took a threatening step toward Alex. "Take your fucking hands off her."

"Noah," Jared warned again as the crowd gathered around them. The bonfire burned bright, the fiery embers sparking like angry fireflies in the dark night sky, casting a flickering spotlight on the scene playing out before them. "You start this shit again, and Donald won't give you any more chances," he bit out harshly, but Noah was too far gone, too far down the road filled with blood and bad memories to walk away.

"I didn't start it." He swiped his tongue over his swollen lip and jutted his chin toward Alex. "He did. I'm just going to finish it." Noah stood there, sizing up his opponent once again, waiting for him to make another move.

Alex looked at Noah, then at his girlfriend, who continued to struggle against his grip. Suspicion moved into his beady eyes as they locked on hers. "What are you protecting this guy for? Do you know him or something?" he asked, his voice slurring slightly.

"We're all just here to have a good time, Alex."

"A good time?" He jerked his head toward Noah, his lips curling with disgust. "That's the good time you want?" Silence hung heavy for a moment, then sweet tits shrugged, everything in what she didn't say answering Alex's question. "This shit ain't worth it." He shoved Dara away, pushed through the crowd and stormed down the beach.

He watched Alex disappear and then turned his attention to Dara. "You okay?"

Big eyes moved over his swollen lip as her two friends came up behind her. "Are you?" she asked.

Noah scrubbed his hand over his jaw. "Your boyfriend throws one hell of a punch."

She took a sip from the cooler her friend handed her, looking at him over the rim of the bottle. She swallowed and licked her lips before saying, "Maybe he's not my boyfriend anymore."

"Is that right?" Noah asked, inching closer and invading her personal space. Damn she smelled good.

"Well, maybe not tonight, anyway." She nibbled her bottom lip, a seductive move Noah figured she'd perfected in front of a mirror, and then slid her gaze over his body.

"You gotta be fucking kidding me." The sound of Jared's voice from behind him pulled Noah's attention away from those luscious lips.

Noah cast him a quick glance and smirked. "What?"

"Like you even have to ask." Shaking his head, Jared disappeared into the crowd, leaving Noah to do what he did best. Fuck everything up.

With the fight over, the crowd went back to partying, and Dara stepped in and closed the small space that remained between them. She went up on her tiptoes, those nice tits of hers pressing into his chest. Reaching up, she feathered her fingertip over his swollen lip. "Does it hurt?"

"Yeah. It hurts like a son of a bitch. But I guess that's to be expected when I use my face to stop a punch."

She puckered those pouty lips of hers and all Noah could think about was how that sexy mouth would feel around his cock.

"You think I should kiss it better?"

Noah grinned. Christ, she made this so easy. "I think that's a good start."

She handed her cooler back to her friends, and gave the cute brunette a knowing smile before she turned back to Noah. With a tip of her head, she gestured behind her. "Maybe we should...you know...go somewhere private."

She didn't need to ask him twice. Noah grabbed her hand and pulled her away from the crowd. Once they were out of sight, near the rocky cliff at the far end of the beach, he stepped into the water and splashed a palm full into his mouth. He sloshed it around to wash away the blood, and then spat it out.

Not wasting any time, he gripped Dara's hips, his cock swelling inside his jeans as he pushed her up against the rock wall. He dipped his head, his lips so close to hers that he could taste the raspberry cooler on her breath. Goddamn she had a mouth made for sucking. He slipped one hand around the back of her neck, the floral scent of her hair filling his nostrils as his eyes latched on her hot mouth.

"So about that kiss," he murmured.

Her tongue flicked out to moisten her bottom lip and ignoring the split on his lip, he crushed his mouth to hers. The pressure stung like a bitch, but he didn't care. He groaned as sensations overcame him, let them push back the memories that came far too close to the surface tonight. His tongue slipped inside to thrash with hers as his hands went to her tits. He palmed them and she moaned, wiggling against him. With his mouth watering for a taste of her nipples, he gripped the hem of her shirt and tugged.

He pulled it over her head and inched back to look at her lace bra. "Sweet," he murmured and she smiled at him, the look on her face telling him she knew she was as sexy as hell and could have whoever she wanted. He was fine with that. She wanted a good time, and tonight he was the guy she'd chosen to provide it. It wasn't his fault she picked a no good loser like him. But some of the townies liked to go slumming during their summer break, and as long as he was getting a piece of ass, he was cool with it.

He reached behind her back, made quick work of the metal hook, and then tossed the bra onto the rocks along with her shirt. Pushing a knee between her legs, he widened them and bent to draw a hard nipple into his mouth.

Her hands raked through his hair and she whimpered. He ignored the pain in his jaw and sucked deep, needing to get lost in her. Her hands moved to his shirt, and she tugged at the material. He reached behind his neck and tugged it over his shoulders, adding it to the pile forming on the rocks. Once he was half naked, she raced those soft fingers over him.

"Nice tat," she whispered, tracing the cross tombstone on his arm.

An uneasy tremble moved through him as she stroked him. He grabbed her hands, put them behind her and lightly brushed the tattoo at the small of her back. "I like yours, too."

She made a move to reach for him again, but he pushed against her, caging her hands between her ass and the rock. "Keep them there," he ordered.

She looked like she was going to protest, but when he released the button on her shorts, and shoved his hand inside, a low moan rose from her throat. His cock throbbed against her thigh and she sucked in a quick breath when he dipped inside her panties to finger her pussy. A whimpering sound bubbled up from her throat.

"Feel good, baby?" he asked.

"So good," she said, bucking against his hand.

He pushed a finger inside her and his mind shut down when he felt her wetness. "Jesus, you're drenched," he growled. He pushed deep, and while she looked so fucking hot in her short shorts, with his hand inside her panties, he couldn't get a good finger bang going with her still dressed.

Panting hard, and keeping a finger inside her, he said, "Take your shorts off."

She pulled her hands out from behind her, pushed her shorts down and wiggled them to her feet. Her pussy tightened around his finger with her movements. With his free hand, Noah pulled them from her ankles and tossed them onto the pile.

Leaning up against the rocks, she spread her legs wide to give him better access, and the sweet scent of her hot pussy hit him like a double shot of rum. The world around him faded, dulled to a hush. He pushed his finger in and out of her, until she was so soaked and ready that all he could think about was ramming his dick into her.

Her hands went to his zipper. "Take yours off too," she said breathlessly. "I want to see your cock."

Noah groaned. Oh yeah, this girl really was all kinds of trouble.

He pulled his finger out of her pussy, tore off his pants, and threw them on top of her clothes. His cock jutted forward, so hard and ready his brain was nearly blank. Jesus, he loved it when his brain shut down. Her gaze dropped, and she made a whimpering sound as she reached for his dick. He nudged his hips forward, offering it to her. It was true he didn't like to be touched, but when a chick wanted to stroke his dick, he damn well made an exception.

"So big," she murmured.

"You like it big, baby?"

"Yeah." She licked her mouth, her hands grasping his cock harder.

Noah swallowed hard. "You want to suck it?"

She gave him a sexy grin that told him how much she liked sucking cock, how good she was at it, before she sank to her knees. The second her mouth wrapped around his crown, he gripped her head with one hand and braced the other on the rock wall behind her. Christ, her hot wet mouth felt so damn good.

"Fuck..."

She moaned around a mouthful of cock, and he rocked into her, hitting the back of her throat. She gagged a little, but continued to try to take him deeper.

"Nice," he murmured, ramming into her.

She licked the long length of him, her tongue running circles around his crown before she plunged forward to take him back in again. She spent a long time working him in and out of her hot mouth, and when he groaned, she cupped his balls. They drew up tight against his body, and knowing he was close to coming in her mouth, he inched back, and hauled her against him, desperate to bury himself inside her.

He gripped her hips, and lifted her until she was sitting on the ledge, shoving his shirt underneath her ass. His fingers bit into her thighs as he widened them. Bending forward to better position himself between her spread legs, he swiped her cunt with his tongue, and she jutted her tits forward as she leaned back, her palms braced on the rock behind her.

Noah grabbed his pants, and pulled a condom from the pocket. He tore into it and rolled the rubber down the long length of cock.

Dara's eyes widened in anticipation as he wrapped one arm around her slim waist for leverage, and positioned his cock at her entrance.

"You ready to fuck?" he asked.

Instead of answering she wiggled her hips, forcing him in an inch.

"Christ," he groaned as her heat wrapped around him. He held her tighter, and in one quick thrust powered into her. She gasped and rubbed her hard nipples against his chest.

He pumped deep, fast, ramming so hard he was sure they were going to punch through the rock wall. She moved with him, and he inched back to look between their bodies as he pulled out, only to sink all the way back inside again. Jesus, she was hot...

He fucked her long and hard, until her body tightened and she made a whimpering sound. A second later her hot cream singed his cock. As her muscles squeezed his dick, she reached for him again, but he pinned her arms to her sides and pumped feverishly. He knew he was being rough, knew he was going to leave her bruised come morning, but there was nothing he could do to slow down. He needed to fuck. He needed to forget. Oh, God, he just needed...

His cock swelled to the point of no return, every nerve in his body alive and on fire. He drove all the way insider her, burying himself balls deep as he let go, splashing his seed into the condom. He threw his head back and growled, concentrating on the explosions rocketing through him. She squeezed him with her cunt, milking every last drop of his release.

Sweat trickled down his brow, and he swiped it away as he strived to catch his breath. Dara shifted and pulled away, his cock slipping out of her. He stood back, water splashing against his heels as he disposed of the rubber. Dara reached for her clothes and pulled them on quickly. Once she was dressed, she jumped from the ledge and grinned up at him.

"Thanks," she said, licking her lips and smoothing down her long blonde hair as her skin glistened with perspiration. "That was fun."

"Yeah," he said, his voice rough, edgy as he reached behind her to grab his pants. She stepped around him, and he said, "I'll guess I'll see you around." He tugged his jeans on and gave a casual roll of his shoulder.

"Sure. I'll be around," she said and then disappeared down the beach, dismissing him like he was nothing but a go nowhere loser, a go-to guy when a girl needed to scratch an itch.

What bothered him the most was that she was right.

ABOUT CAT

New York Times and *USA today* Bestselling author, Cathryn Fox/Cat Kalen is a wife, mom, sister, daughter, and friend. She loves dogs, sunny weather, anything chocolate (she never says no to a brownie) pizza and red wine. She has two teenagers who keep her busy with their never ending activities, and a husband who is convinced he can turn her into a mixed martial arts fan. Cathryn can never find balance in her life, is always trying to find time to go to the gym, can never keep up with emails, Facebook or Twitter and tries to write page-turning books that her readers will love.

Connect with Cathryn:
Newsletter
https://app.mailerlite.com/webforms/landing/c1f8n1
Twitter: https://twitter.com/writercatfox
Facebook:
https://www.facebook.com/AuthorCathrynFox?ref=hl
Blog: http://cathrynfox.com/blog/
Goodreads:
https://www.goodreads.com/author/show/91799.Cathryn_Fox

ABOUT CAT

Pinterest http://www.pinterest.com/catkalen/

www.ingramcontent.com/pod-product-compliance
Lightning Source LLC
Chambersburg PA
CBHW030648110726
47901CB00002B/614